W9-AMQ-081

**This book was
presented to
Mount Tamalpais
School Library
in honor of the
birthday of**

Liz Madjlessi

this **7th** day of *July* 19**94**

A Bowl
of Mischief

Ellen Kindt McKenzie

❦ ❦ ❦

A Bowl of Mischief

Henry Holt and Company • *New York*

First edition
Published by Henry Holt and Company, Inc.,
115 West 18th Street, New York, New York 10011.
Published simultaneously in Canada by Fitzhenry & Whiteside Ltd.,
91 Granton Drive, Richmond Hill, Ontario L4B 2N5.

Library of Congress Cataloging-in-Publication Data
McKenzie, Ellen Kindt.
A bowl of mischief / Ellen Kindt McKenzie.
Summary: An abandoned child in the desert is found and taught
by a holy man whose teachings he mischievously resists, only to
regret it years later when he needs that wisdom as he finds
himself in a battle of wits with a fearsome villain.
ISBN 0-8050-2090-X (alk. paper)
[1. Adventure and adventurers—Fiction.]   I. Title.
PZ7.M478676Bo   1992
[Fic]—dc20   92-24246

Printed in the United States of America
on acid-free paper. ∞

10 9 8 7 6 5 4 3 2 1

To my sister, Joann Kindt

Contents

A Bowl of Mischief

1

A Scamp and an Imp
and the Old Faquir

There was once, in a most ancient of ancient countries, a boy. His name was Ranji. He was a scamp, and an imp, and so full of mischief that he might not have lived long had it not been for an old faquir.

A faquir is one who has lived so long he has learned that true happiness lies in wanting nothing. This faquir, whose name was Phufadia, was so old that he had gone beyond even that. He had given up wanting so long ago that wisdom had replaced the lack of desire. Thus he did not even desire not to desire. This left him free to learn all there was to learn and to enjoy everything.

All that he had learned he told to the boy, Ranji.

"It is better to build than to destroy," the old man said as he watched the child push a stick beneath the house of sand his playmates had made. The boy jumped on the stick and shouted gleefully to see the sand fly into the air.

"It is better to love than to hate," he sighed as Ranji

1

howled a vengeance of fists against his playmates and wept over his defeat in the scuffle that followed the destruction of the sand house.

"It is better to cherish than to kill," Phufadia murmured as Ranji, still snuffling, stamped furiously on a line of ants that ran to and fro between their nest and a drop of honey.

"For the larger and stronger to destroy the smaller and weaker is the work of a bully," he went on while Ranji dribbled sand into the holes of the ants' nest. "The weak come to know hatred, and the strong swagger when they should be ashamed."

Phufadia picked up the boy and carried him to the river's edge. "Early on I wept over the follies of men who had no understanding of these precepts," he continued. "Then I tried to laugh, but though I could laugh at some, I could not laugh at them all."

The old man plopped the boy into the shallow water and rinsed the tear-streaked dirt from his face and the sand from his hair. After plastering cool mud on the ant bites on Ranji's ankles, he sighed once more. "Try as I have, I cannot laugh at the greed of those who cause misery in others. But I have learned to laugh at myself, especially for taking in such a scamp as you." He watched Ranji splash in the water, and finished with, "The follies of others I accept, though I keep hoping for better. Someday I may even hope for you."

He told this and more—for his knowledge was vast—to Ranji and to anyone else who came along.

But Phufadia's learning was imparted with such a twinkle of the eye that none took him too seriously. As for Ranji, he was so busy thinking of more mischief that he did not try to understand what Phufadia was talking about. The boy let the words either fly past his ears or nestle into that part of his mind which stored forgotten wisdom.

What Ranji did pay attention to was Phufadia's dancing on burning coals or twisting himself into a tangle as impossible as three intertwining grape tendrils.

It was fun to see the old faquir do magic. Phufadia could place a bean under one half of a walnut shell and make it appear under the other half. He could pull a dove from a woman's ear. He could tuck a small blue silken scarf between thumb and forefinger of his empty fist and draw out yards and yards of green and yellow and orange and purple scarf from beneath the little finger. He could toss a golden coin into the air without its ever coming down again or, if the matter called for it, cause it to fall in a shower of ten golden coins.

He was not only a wise man, but a clever one as well.

But Ranji was such a scamp and spent so much of his time being a boy that he paid no more attention to how Phufadia did what he did than he listened to what the old faquir had to say.

When he was old enough to notice something other

than himself, Ranji did see that other boys had either a father or a mother or, quite frequently, one of each. It seemed to him that Phufadia was too old to be his father and he certainly was not his mother. One day, as they squatted on the ground and shared a bowl of rice begged from the woman who raised chickens, Ranji asked the old faquir, "Are you my father?"

"No," Phufadia told him.

"Then why do I live with you?" asked the boy.

"Because I found you and have reared you the best I could, which is what a father should do."

"Where did you find me?" Ranji then asked.

"In the great desert of the north. I had gone there to meditate and gain wisdom. Just as I was about to gain the final understanding, I heard you crying. I hunted all over until I found you under a barren thornbush that grew behind a tall rock. If you had remained silent, I never would have found you, but you were howling so, there was nothing to be seen of you but your mouth. I knew at once that you were born a scamp and an imp and so full of mischief that, in despair, your mother had left you for me to find. For if she had kept you, your nine brothers and sisters would have had to put up with your tricks forever and not a one of them would have been able to make a good marriage."

To this the old man added, with his usual twinkle, "Alas for all my seeking! I found *you* instead of wisdom."

"Where are my mother and my brothers and sisters?" Ranji asked.

"I looked but never found them," Phufadia told him. "Certainly they all made good marriages and lived happily ever after."

Ranji did not doubt his word for a minute because the old man always told the truth. He was glad for his family's good fortune and asked about them no more. He did not miss what he had never had.

Perhaps the old faquir should not have told Ranji *all* of these truths, for the one that Ranji took most to heart was that he was a scamp and an imp and full of mischief. Knowing this, he often brought both himself and Phufadia to grief.

Phufadia would sigh and say, "If you would listen for five minutes, there are things I could teach you that would keep you out of trouble. Beyond that, someday you will have to look after yourself, and you should know how."

But Ranji did not pay attention. The old man was always giving forth words of wisdom, and Ranji did not care to hear two more of them. Besides, he could not sit still for the five minutes it would take to learn. He was off and into a new mischief and a greater trouble.

One day Ranji poured molasses over the sandals of the elders while they purified themselves in the river.

"Such behavior calls for punishment!" cried the outraged villagers. "The father must be punished for rearing such a mischievous boy and the son for being such a scamp!"

As Phufadia and Ranji had nothing but their freedom and the bowls they used in begging rice, both were taken from them. The old faquir and the boy were sentenced to prison for a week with nothing to eat and only stale water to drink.

"How long is a week?" Ranji asked anxiously.

"A week lasts a full seven days, and seven nights as well," Phufadia told him.

"That is forever!" the boy cried.

"No. It will pass," the old man said.

But it still worried Ranji, and with good reason. Indeed, the boy was not happy for a single minute of that time, because there was no mischief to make in the bare little room. The barred window was too high in the wall to look through. Worse, he was hungry every day from dawn to dusk and every night from dusk to dawn. All day every day he grumbled, and for all but one night of that week he dreamed of his dinner.

The first night Ranji dreamed of a bowl of rice. The second night he dreamed of a bowl of rice seasoned with cinnamon. The third night he dreamed of a bowl of rice and eggplant seasoned with cumin. The fourth night he dreamed of rice and fish baked over hot coals with a delicate sauce of mangoes and onions seasoned with cardamom and cumin and ginger. The fifth night he dreamed of a roasted bird filled with rice and hot peppers and woke to to find his middle burning on the inside as if he had swallowed twenty of the little peppers. On the sixth night he dreamed that a banquet, with dish after dish of seasoned rice and toasted nuts, succulent fish with tender vegetables, and juicy grapes and slices of ripe melon, was set before him, none of which he was allowed to touch. He woke crying from hunger.

On the seventh night he had a vision of a beautiful lady. She told him that she was his grandmother and had come to help him.

"Your mischief has caused your bowl to be empty of rice," she told him. "If you will learn what Phufadia has to teach you, you will never go hungry again."

That was the end of the week of imprisonment, and Ranji was so hungry he was willing to promise anything, if only he might have a bowl of steamed rice.

Phufadia, none the worse at all for his seven days of fasting, smiled gently upon hearing of his dream and said, "Your dream was a wise grandmother."

When they came out of the prison, Phufadia begged two bowls of rice from the chicken lady's three-legged pot. After they had eaten their fill, the old faquir taught Ranji how to hide a bean under the half shell of a walnut and make it disappear, only to reappear under the other half of the shell.

Ranji learned to do it in less than five minutes.

"This is more fun than I expected learning to be!" he cried. "But how will it keep me from being hungry?"

"Simple enough! If you have to shell the walnut and

can remember where the bean is, you will always have that much to eat." The old faquir winked.

Ranji did not see where that would fill the kind of hunger he had learned of. "One walnut and a single bean isn't much," he grumbled.

"Well then, perhaps we will find a way of making your mischief fill the bowl with rice," said Phufadia.

Did the old man know of a way to make a bowl of rice with cinnamon and honey appear beneath a walnut shell? The boy burned to know what else Phufadia would teach him.

2

Traveling

he next day Phufadia said to Ranji, "We shall travel for a time."

They bid good-bye to the village where they had been imprisoned and took the road that crisscrossed that ancient country, a land so old its primordial name has been forever lost in the rust of distant time.

As they journeyed, Phufadia taught Ranji all that he himself knew how to do. The boy practiced his skill on the road and in every village they came to.

"Aaiii!" cried a girl when Ranji drew a coin from the back of her neck.

"How did you do that?" cried a child, peering under the empty walnut shell.

"Tricks!" snorted the gambler when the deck of cards flew through the air and fell with his chosen card lying on top. Ranji grinned.

Phufadia continued to teach the boy.

"Here is how to stuff clothes with straw to make a puppet as large as yourself. Fasten its feet to your toes and dance with it. Here is how to make a mask of

your own face. If you do this, you have a demon's
face. If you change it so, you have a tiger's face."

Ranji slipped the mask of a tiger over his head and
snarled.

"When your voice is lower, people will believe you
are truly a tiger," Phufadia told him.

All of this Ranji learned with no trouble because it
was very much the same as being a scamp and an imp
and had a wonderful sense of mischief about it. In no
time he was as quick of hand as old Phufadia, and
soon after was even quicker.

"Where did you get that pigeon?" a child asked.

"I had it up my sleeve," Ranji told him.

This made it all the more mystifying, for Ranji had
no sleeve at all to his ragged shirt.

Phufadia taught the boy other things. He taught
him how to sit with his knees behind his ears and his
chin resting on his toes. He taught him how to walk
over burning coals without feeling the heat. He taught
him how to balance on a tightrope. He taught him
how to play the flute and how to dance. He taught
him how to lie flat on his back and then bring himself
to float in the air six inches above the ground. Between times he told him an endless number of unfor-
gettable tales.

All this Ranji learned as they traveled back and
forth from east to west across that ancient country. It
was a vast country made up of many little kingdoms
and states and sultanates and duchies and democra-

cies and empires and superdoms and provinces. Each state had its king or its president or its sultan or its prime minister or its rajah or its emperor or its superus or its satrap.

Ranji and Phufadia came to do their tricks before the dusty tents of the camel drivers and in the marketplaces of the villages and in the streets of the cities and in the courts of each and all of the states they passed through. From the least beggar in the street to the mightiest emperor in his jewel-studded marble palace they provided entertainment for all.

So they earned their way from east to west and west to east as they traveled, moving slowly from the very south toward the north of the land. All of this time Ranji was happy.

"You were right about learning," he said one day. "Ever since I learned how to do these tricks, we have never been hungry. It must be that the more of them I learn, the more we will have for dinner."

Phufadia nodded. "It is possible. But you must be careful not to learn to do so much that you grow fat from eating the rewards. It is hard to fold your legs behind your ears if you are too fat. There are some things you should think about."

"Thinking would make me sit still and grow fat," the boy protested.

"Perhaps," Phufadia said, "but all the same . . ." Then, as he often did, Phufadia talked about life and wisdom and happiness.

Ranji preferred to learn how to do things than to listen to words of wisdom. So, as usual, he paid little attention to the old faquir's musings. It was far better to delight in his own quickness and cleverness than brood over the fog of the old man's contemplations. He quickly stored Phufadia's ponderings with all other forgotten things where they would not get in the way. His mind clear of nonsense, the boy smiled as he deceived others with his fluttering hands and amused them with his glib tongue and whirling body.

Best of all, there were always enough coins for fruit or rice. Often even *pooris,* those delicious little puffed rounds of bread that Ranji loved, were given to them after his performance. What more could a boy ask for?

In this way seven years passed happily.

But in all that time Ranji never forgot the hunger of his seven days of imprisonment. Each day, after eating his bowl of spicy *dal* and curd or rice and vegetables with a sweet, tart sauce of mangoes and raisins and almonds, he would remember. Then he would pat his middle in contentment and say, "There is nothing better than a full stomach."

"It brings comfort to the body," Phufadia would admit. "But that is not all that matters."

After a day of walking and performing, Ranji preferred sleeping to listening. So, with his hunger filled, he was careful not to ask what else might matter. Phufadia, seeing the boy's eyes close, would sit cross-legged on his mat and think about what mattered.

For the moment what mattered to both of them was that they were happy together. At this point in his meditating, Phufadia's eyes would close too, and his thoughts would come to him in ways that, on the next morning, left him wondering about their meanings. So it went, day after day and night after night, until they found themselves almost at the very north of that ancient land.

One evening, after finishing his meal, Ranji said as usual, "There is nothing better than a full stomach." Without thinking, he added, "It keeps my heart perfectly content."

Phufadia said, "A stomach grows full with giving food to it, but a heart grows full with giving things from it."

"Mmm," Ranji murmured. He had already closed his eyes.

"A man with a full stomach is only half a man," the old faquir persisted. "A man with a full stomach and an empty heart is worse than no man . . ."

Ranji opened one eye.

". . . because he is an unhappy man," Phufadia went on, "and an unhappy man makes others unhappy."

Ranji yawned. "I must be more than a man," he murmured. "I have a full stomach and I am happy."

Upon hearing Phufadia say "Your full stomach is not what makes you happy," he closed his eye again and fell asleep.

Phufadia continued to sit upon his mat, but he did not meditate, as had become his habit on this journey.

He sat with his eyes open all the night long. Only when the sun came up did he close them and lay himself down on his mat.

When the boy woke, he saw at once that though the old faquir's body lay upon the mat, Phufadia himself had left both it and Ranji.

It was then that he understood what Phufadia had meant by those last words, for Ranji was miserably unhappy. Whether he mourned by eating his fill or mourned with fasting, still he mourned. His heart, heavy with sorrow, had nothing to do with his stomach. He wept and was lonely as he had never been in his life.

"I always thought that you were too old to die," he sobbed. "And I can remember only one thing you said about dying.

"You said, *The very young never worry about death, because they believe they will live forever.* Which of course I will. And then you said, *The very old welcome it as a peaceful sleep.* Which you have done. *But those in the middle,* you said, *those who have suddenly discovered that they are not immortal, live in terror of death, for they have been so busy gathering wealth that they have tasted nothing of life's true joy and so are in no way ready to die.* Which had nothing to do with either of us.

"But see? I remember a great many of your words. Even so, none of them mean anything, because they say nothing about being lonely!"

Ranji wept again that he had not listened more carefully to all that the old faquir had said. Surely there was more than that to bring him comfort!

Then one night he dreamed. In his dream the beautiful grandmother who had come at the end of his seven days' imprisonment again appeared.

"Grandmother!" Ranji cried out in his dream.

She brushed his forehead with her fingertips and said gently, "You must carry the ashes of Phufadia to the great desert that lies to the north and scatter them under the thornbush where he found you."

The boy still had the ashes of the old faquir because he had been unable to decide where to bury or scatter them. Now he knew. As her first piece of advice—that he must learn from Phufadia—had brought him happiness, Ranji determined to do as he was told. He took up the jar that held what remained of Phufadia and, though his heart was still heavy, set out at once for the great desert to the north.

3

Ranji Hears of the Mighty Superus

anji soon arrived at the border of the last small domain that lay between him and the great desert.

"I must travel through this country in order to come to the great desert that lies beyond it. There I must perform a sacred duty," he told the guards as his reason for being there.

"That may be as you say, but the Superus who rules here demands a careful examination of all who enter his country," the guards told him. "We must know what you bring with you."

They soon found that the boy carried little.

"Why only seven coins? No matter. You cannot use these in the country of the Superus," said one tall guard, pocketing the small handful of coppers Ranji had earned from his last performance.

"Scarcely enough clothes to keep you clean," said another, handing back the slight bundle of shirt and pants, much too small for the guard himself.

"You need only three of these six *pooris*. They are

16

already soft—*baasi*—and the other three would dry out before you could eat them," said a third, relieving the boy of half of his dinner.

"Playing cards? But they have all the same face! What use are they? And these scarves? You carry useless things," a fourth informed him disdainfully.

A few walnuts and some dried beans were also left to Ranji.

"What is in the jar? Why ashes?" he was asked.

"They are of a holy man. It is my duty to scatter them beneath a certain thornbush," Ranji explained.

"You may pass through at once," he was told by all.

As he put what was left him back into the sack, the tallest guard, whose beard curled under his chin, advised him, "You'll do well to cross this country quickly, for the Highest Most Excellent Superus is not kind to beggars. If the *poori* and dried beans and walnuts are all that you have to eat, guard them carefully lest they be stolen from you. Either way, you will find yourself very hungry before you come to the great desert."

"Thank you, but I shall earn my way," Ranji told him.

"There will be little to earn," said the man. "The people have nothing for payment, and the Superus does not like to share his dinner. You should turn back and not risk being hanged for bringing so little to eat with you, for it means you will either beg or steal."

But Ranji was determined to scatter the ashes of his beloved faquir under the thornbush, whatever it cost him.

"I am neither a beggar nor a thief. I shall go on," he said.

The guard touched the fingertips of one hand to his forehead and nodded soberly. "As you will."

Thus Ranji entered the Superdom of the Highest Most Excellent Superus.

It was indeed a poor country. The road was deeply rutted, and there was scarcely a tree to give shade along the way. The fields to both left and right were bare or showed crops so meager, it looked as if nothing would be gained by harvesting them. The boy wondered if a plague of grasshoppers had come through and eaten everything down to the soil and rock. He saw few people, and these only in far-off fields where the dust rose around them as they bent their backs to hoe and plow with not even a bullock to help them.

Ranji walked half the day and then sat down beside the ditch and ate one *poori*. He was hungry enough that he could have eaten all three, but he remembered Phufadia's telling him, "Always keep something aside. You will be hungry again soon enough." So he heeded both the words of the faquir and those of the guard. After carefully wrapping the remaining two *pooris* in his second ragged shirt, he went on.

The air above the road and fields shimmered and quivered under the hot sun, so Ranji was never sure that what he saw was a temple or the reflection of a pile of stones, or a lake or a piece of the sky come down to lie on the ground. He longed for the shade of a tree where he might nap, but there was none and so he kept walking.

He walked until the sun hung low over the blue hills and shone red through the golden dust of the air.

"I must have a tree to sit in for the night," he told himself, "for if a tiger wandered out of the jungle, it would easily see me in this open land. A jackal could certainly find me. A snake might even swallow me."

None of these thoughts comforted him, but there was no magic he knew that could make a tree grow for him. All afternoon he had walked toward a line of hills. Now he was close enough so that, by the low sun that lighted their rounded tops, he saw the towers and walls of a great fortress. It stretched across and down the sides and into the shadows of the highest hill. He would be safe there.

"If the sun is down, they won't let me through the gates," Ranji murmured, and hurried on as fast as he could. But he could not go fast enough. When the last of the shining disk slipped behind the world, the boy had come only to the foot of the hills. To his great relief, he found a small village there. At least he might earn a bowl of rice and a mat to sleep on.

His first look showed him not much less than other poor villages he and Phufadia had passed through. A few houses made of brick with no mortar huddled one against another. Others made of sticks and mud straggled along the road. Here and there a tent of goatskin offered a family shelter. The rest of the dwellings were open affairs of poles with sagging roofs of gray thatch.

But it was the people who startled the boy. Their faces showed a gaunt look of hunger such as he had never seen. Suddenly the voice of Phufadia came to him as if the old man were speaking into his ear: *The greatest poverty always dwells side by side with the greatest wealth.*

He remembered the old faquir's telling him this when they had seen many beggars on the steps of the palace of a great city. Why it should be so, Ranji had never asked. But never, even in the poorest parts of the richest cities, had he beheld such misery as there was here. The fortress that rose above them must hold the greatest wealth the world had ever known!

The youth stood in the middle of the road and looked at those who had gathered around him, some two dozen or so folk all in rags. Old men, young men, old women, young women—some with babies in their arms—small children, middle-size children, a yellow dog with a curly tail and its ribs showing, all gathered around him much the same as the people had in any village he had come through.

But how could he ask a supper from them? They were so thin! Once more he remembered advice of the old faquir. When the boy had been complaining about the difficulty of a certain trick, Phufadia had said, "You learn in order to give delight. Delight and pleasure are always welcomed by one and all—by those who have nothing as much as by those who have everything. The overfed forget their indigestion and the underfed forget their hunger."

"I . . . ah . . . hmmm." Ranji cleared his throat. "I bring you delight. The very best I know."

He reached into his sack and began a performance like none he had ever given. Never had his hand been so quick nor his tongue so glib nor his feet so nimble. The village people first watched with sad eyes. Then mouths fell agape, then they smiled, then they stamped with pleasure.

When he had finished, the oldest man in the village embraced him.

"You have given us as much as a full bowl of rice!" he exclaimed. "In payment, we beg you share our evening meal with us."

Ranji wondered what that might be. He went with the people to the the end of the village where they gathered in a circle around an old blind woman. She tended a three-legged pot that boiled over a small fire.

"We are all here now," said the man who had invited Ranji.

The blind woman thrust her hand into a sack and brought up a single handful of rice. With a wooden spoon in the other hand she stirred the rice into the boiling water.

"It is our evening meal," said the man. "When the rice has cooked, each of us gets an equal number of grains. You will have a share."

The handful of rice would not make even one bowl, and it must feed the whole village and himself! Ranji's heart turned in his chest. Never had he felt so ashamed at accepting food.

"Here," he said, and brought out the dried beans from his pack. "I need only one of these." And he dropped all but one into the boiling water with the rice.

Then he searched out the walnuts.

"I need only the shells," he said, and with the help of a child with thin fingers and a face too small for her dark eyes, he cracked the walnuts with a stone and took the meats from the shells.

When the rice and the beans were cooked, the portions were carefully doled out: thirty-seven grains of rice and one bean for each man, woman, and child. Ranji's walnuts were broken and shared equally.

Ranji then brought out his two rounds of *poori* and divided them so that all the villagers had at least one mouthful of the bread.

For some reason this seemed to content Ranji—if not his stomach, at least his heart—for he had given all he had. The villagers too looked happy. The rest of the evening was passed in his singing and playing the flute and telling tales and putting on the tiger mask and snarling, all for the lovely mixture of delight and terror that this brought. After that he listened to old and new tales of the village life.

"Why do you stay here?" Ranji asked at last. "You say it was once rich, but that now the soil is poor. You are not getting enough to eat from it. Why don't you go to a place that is more fertile?"

"Alas," an old man told him, "the soil was indeed rich, and it would be again if we could let part of it lie fallow while we tilled another part. But the Most Excellent Superus, whose fortress and palace cover the top of the highest hill, demands that we raise three crops a year, and there is little ground that will nourish that much."

"Why does he want so much?" Ranji asked.

"He has a vast appetite," a woman burst out. "He eats all that we can raise, and more besides. There is as little as nothing left for the rest of us. It is not fair!"

"Hush!" her husband warned her. "You must not speak so about the Superus. There are always ears that hear everything we say."

"He is otherwise good to us," the woman mumbled. "It has been some time since he has had one of us hanged." She then fell silent.

Ranji asked no more, but he wondered how one man could have so prodigious an appetite.

At last everyone grew sleepy, and Ranji was happy to accept the offer of a place to lie beneath a thatched roof. Tired as he was, he lay wakeful, for though his heart was full, his belly was still empty. Besides that, he could not help but know that the bellies of the villagers were emptier than his own, and the great dark eyes and tiny hands of the little girl who had helped crack the walnuts haunted him.

"Phufadia," he whispered. "As soon as I have scattered your ashes under the thornbush, I will find some way of helping these people."

Then he grew sleepy. "I shall be careful to walk around the royal palace of that High and Most Excellent Majesty," he murmured, and fell asleep, thankful that he would not be long in the country of the Great Superus.

But in the morning Ranji was wakened by the sound of a brass horn.

"The traveler is called to the court of the Highest Most Excellent Superus!" announced a voice. "He must come at once to perform his magic tricks, or he will be hanged."

Ranji sat up and rubbed the sleep from his eyes. He was the only traveler in the village. There was nothing for him to do but go with the messenger.

4

The Highest Most Excellent Superus

anji followed the messenger, who wore a cream-colored turban and ragged trousers and rode a tall elephant. Through the dust raised by the elephant the boy could see the high red-brick walls and many towers of the fortress. It covered the tops of not one but two hills, and its walls stretched down the sides of both. It was immense, and the road to it wound endlessly upward. Ranji felt that he must have climbed at least a thousand and seven stairs, and there were yet a thousand and seven to go. He longed that he too might ride on the head of the lurching, swaying beast. But such was not his luck, and he plodded along in the dust behind it, feeling smaller than he ever had in all his life.

At last the youth and the messenger crossed a bridge over two moats, one with water where crocodiles swam and one with grass where tigers roamed. Eleven guards allowed them to pass under the archway of a mighty gate. On and on they went within the fort, through flowering gardens and wide courtyards, to the very back of it all, where rose the palace of the Highest Most Excellent Superus.

Now in his travels with Phufadia, Ranji had seen not only poor villages but many great cities and strong fortresses. He had seen beautiful temples and high monuments and wide courts of justice and jewel-encrusted palaces. His mouth had often hung open at the number and the elegance of gardens and courtyards and halls and chambers. He had performed in magnificent throne rooms, with windows screened by filigrees of white marble, and walls engraved with the most delicate designs, and columns covered with the carved figures of many creatures. He had gawked at basins and pools and jars the height of a man, all filled to overflowing with diamonds and sapphires, emeralds and rubies.

Ranji knew how lavish a palace could be.

And so he looked for such magnificence here. But though he saw ample rooms and columns and archways and lintels with wondrous beings and delightful creatures carved upon them with the greatest skill, he saw only jars tipped on their sides with nothing spilling from them and basins with but a scant handful of opals or agates lying in the bottom. It appeared to him that jewels had even been dug from many of the tracings on the walls.

The people of the village must have been mistaken, Ranji thought. This mighty Superus is as poor as they are.

But if his eyes showed him loss of fortune, his nose spoke to him of riches that made his mouth water and his eyes tear. Ranji inhaled deeply and licked his chops. Oh, what a feast must dwell in this palace!

Finally they passed beneath an archway, and Ranji saw before him a sight from which he could not take his eyes. In a vast room, this one lavish with jewels, a magnificent table extending from wall to wall was spread with mounds of food in a countless number of dishes. Silver platters and golden bowls, copper plates and sauceboats of brass, porcelain trays and salvers, woven baskets and wicker hampers, earthen casseroles and clay jugs. All were heaped and piled and brimming and replete and filled and overflowing and laden and garnished with a display of such savory delicacies as Ranji had never imagined. The delectable fragrance of spices and herbs floated to his nose and made him quite faint, for he had had little enough supper and no breakfast at all.

However, he was allowed scarcely a glance and certainly not a bite. He was hurried past the table and forced to his knees before that Majesty who was Lord and King and Rajah and Emperor and everything else that might have a noble title. All of these rolled into one, he was—the Highest Mightiest Most Excellent Superus.

This Superus sat upon a pillowed throne of red marble and stared at Ranji.

Ranji had but as fleeting a glimpse of the man as

he had had of the table, for not only was he forced to
his knees, but his head was bowed to the floor and
held there. Yet with that single glance Ranji remembered that the people of the village had not spoken of
jewels. They had spoken of a prodigious appetite, and
he understood at once why there was no food for
them.

The Superus was the fattest man Ranji had ever
seen. He was so fat, he bulged over the edges of his
throne. He overflowed in giant mounds from pate to
jowls to belly to thighs to feet. The vision hung in the
boy's mind and wiped out any other thought Ranji
might have had while he kneeled with his nose touching the floor. And so he remained until the voice of
the Superus came to his ears.

"Stand up and tell me why you are here."

"O Most Superous of All Superuses!" said Ranji,
who was now allowed to scramble to his feet and then
again bow low. "You are indeed a marvel of a S-s-s-
super! Surely no man in the world has ever been or
will ever be so superior!" All the time he spoke, he
marveled greatly at the overwhelming size of the Superus. For he was also tall, and he towered on his
throne as well as overflowed it, like a stupendous
statue.

"What do you know of me?" growled the Superus.
"I have never laid eyes on you in all my life."

Ranji had to swallow before he answered, for his
mouth was watering from the spicy scents that wafted
to his nose from the table behind him.

"I come from a faraway part of the world, your Majestic Majesty, and have heard only rumors of you. But since I arrived in your country, I have heard nothing but talk of you. Your name is in the mouth of everyone! I had to come and see for myself if this m-m-mighty ruler was what everyone said he was. And now that I have beheld you with my own eyes, I see indeed that they spoke the truth. But, oh, ah! Their words in no way touched the reality of your being!"

Ranji prayed his meaning would not be asked into, for he told only a half truth. Again words of Phufadia leaped to his thoughts from that part of his mind which had always stored forgotten things: *A half truth is the worst kind of lie, for it is far more devious and destructive than a truly honest lie.*

Ranji waited fearfully, but his words seemed to have flattered the Superus. The Mighty One grunted. "Is that all you have come for? To look at me?"

"Oh, no! I was bidden to come and show all that I have to your Gr-gr-gracious Majesty. I am an entertainer and a magician. I have come to offer the best of my humble skill for your amusement."

"I am seldom amused," said the Superus, glowering at him. "Those who say they will amuse me and do not do so are hanged for my pleasure. It is the last entertainment I ask of them. So. Make me laugh."

Ranji swallowed again. But this time his mouth was dry. If he had been hungry because he had missed his breakfast, his appetite instantly disappeared with the words of the Superus.

He nodded and bowed low. Ranji then performed all of his easier magic. The Superus did not appear amused. The boy went on with more, wondering if he should not keep some of it back, especially the flaring of the black powder that he had so little of. The Superus was not impressed. Ranji danced and juggled, and still the Superus did not smile.

Perhaps this was because all the while the Mighty Superus watched, delicacies were brought before him and fed to him one after another by seven men. This they did because the Superus was so fat, he could not reach around his belly to pick up his fork. Indeed, if a fork had been given to him to hold, he could not have brought it to his mouth. It took four men to feed him and three to wipe away the sauce from his lips and the grease spots from his vest.

Ranji once more grew hungry with seeing the Superus eat. Again his mouth watered, but he could not stop his magic act for fear that he might be hanged. Finally he began telling some of the best and wittiest of the tales he knew. At the last of these, one about a man who was so thin he could tap his ribs with a mallet and produce the sound of tuned drums over his empty belly, the Superus laughed.

Alas.

If it had stopped there, there would have been no problem. But with his laugh the Mighty Majestic One took in a crumb that tickled his throat and brought on a spell of coughing. The coughs of the Superus were so mighty that the walls of the palace trembled and the marble filigree of the windows cracked. The ground shook so that the table legs chattered. Plates of soup and spiced meats leaped to the floor and skittered across it. Huge jardinieres rocked back and forth, lamps tipped over, and the chandeliers swayed until all the ministers and servants dove beneath the table lest the ceiling fall.

Ranji ran to the table, seized a carafe of water, and rushed to the side of the Superus. He thumped him on the back until the coughing eased, then gave him water to sip and wiped away the tears that had come to the ruler's eyes.

At last all was calm.

The Superus cleared his throat and spoke to Ranji.

"I will keep you with me forever. Be entertaining, but not too funny; witty, but not laughably so; clever, but not overly amusing. In return you will have all you want to eat. But if you ever make me laugh again, I will have you hanged."

5

The Kitchen of the Superus

"Oh, ah, aaiii! What have I come into?" Ranji asked himself as he wandered through the palace of the Superus. He was following his nose, but at the same time gazing at the marble walls, which should have been jewel encrusted. He remembered that only the great throne-and-dining room of the Superus was so ornamented. Puzzled, he peered into the basins that were almost empty of gems and shook his head as he stared at the chipped marble of the walls.

"The Superus eats them—the jewels," a serving boy whispered to him as he hurried by.

"What do you mean, eats them?" Ranji called, but the boy had turned a corner and did not come back to explain. The youth went on.

Ranji's nose soon showed his feet the way to the kitchen. There he found twenty cooks, each with an apprentice, each with twenty huge kettles and braziers, each preparing twenty dishes of his own invention.

"Not for you! All for the noonday meal of the

Superus," he was told by a cook with three chins, who frowned and wagged a finger at him. "We may eat none of it ourselves."

"That is so," said the cook's apprentice, who was busy grinding cardamom seeds to a powder with mortar and pestle. Ranji could not help but notice that the lad was as roly-poly as his master. Unlike his master, his grin was wide. "We may eat none of it, but there is one thing we must do."

"And that is taste it," said a second rotund cook, waving a ladle.

"Nothing can go to the Superus that has not been tasted," added a third, who was rubbing pinches of saffron into a pot of rice.

"As there are four hundred dishes being prepared, there is more than we can taste." A fourth cook, round as the moon, grated a nutmeg.

"So all in the fortress—from the seventeen lifters who move the Mighty Superus to his bed, to the least apprentice in the stable of the elephants—must help taste the dishes we have created," a fifth, with as many chins, put in between sips from a wide wooden spoon.

"So it is that none here are ever hungry," added the sixth, who sniffed the steaming aroma of a simmering kettle and smacked his lips.

"And then there are the leftovers," said the seventh, a tear running down his face from chopping onions.

"The whole fortress dines on them, for the Superus must have the table laden with more than even he can

eat. He wishes to be sure there will always be more."
The eighth cook lifted a cleaver and brought it down
with a swift chop.

"The whole fortress cannot eat it all at all," mourned
the ninth cook.

"Would you care to taste?" eleven more cooks asked
Ranji, each holding out a spoon or fork or knife or
skewer or ladle with a tidbit for the boy to sample.

Ranji was more than willing to taste. Taking the
offering of the tenth cook, a chunk of eggplant drip-
ping with sauce, he popped it into his mouth. His eyes
rolled up and he smiled.

"I hear the Superus eats even the jewels from the
walls," he said, patting his stomach and accepting
another taste. "How do you prepare them? What kind
of sauce do you use?"

"Ah, that is just a manner of speaking," the eleventh
cook told him. "Though we take everything they raise,
the peasants of the village below the fortress raise
neither the amount nor the variety needed to feed the
Mighty One. We buy the most exotic of delicacies from
far away—so far that it is very expensive to bring them.
Since the peasants have no money for taxes, the jewels
are all that is left now to pay for such things."

"As the Superus never leaves his throne room or his
bedroom, he does not see that the gems are gone,"
sighed the twelfth cook. "What else can we do? We
would be hanged if we did not serve him something
different every meal."

"Ah." Ranji nodded and took yet another taste. Of course there was no way he could savor each of the four hundred dishes being prepared. But he did his best, and then went back to wandering through the palace, this time looking for a place where he might nap after having eaten so well.

* * *

That evening he waited with the others who were to provide the evening's entertainment for the Superus.

"My name is Chahansa," whispered a boy who sat beside him. "My friends and I dance for the Superus. We work very hard because the Mighty One must always be amused. Also, he must always have something new or we will be hanged. It would be very difficult if I did not love to dance. I hope you love what you do. You too must always be careful to have something new every time you come before him."

"Oh, it is fun for me," Ranji said. "I like the surprise that comes to people's faces when I do what I do." Then he grew thoughtful. He was not used to doing something new each day. He was used to having a new audience each day. Thankful he was for being warned, and thankful too that he had not shown all of his tricks to the Superus. "I shall keep aside four of my best tricks and four of my best stories for a day when I might not be able to think up new ones," he told himself.

"You have saved my life," he said to Chahansa. "If ever I can do the same for you, I will." As Chahansa rose to his feet to join the other dancers, Ranji called after him, "You are my friend forever!"

Then Ranji listened with charmed ears to the music of the sitar and the flute, his spine tingling to the beat of the tabla. His heart swelled with excitement as he peered around the tall column of the archway and watched the movement of the crimson-, gold-, and azure-clad dancers. He prickled all over from the lifting of a toe or the rolling of an eye with the shaking of silver ankle bells, and to the leaping, whirling, twirling wonder of the dancers flying through the air. Besides that, the youngest and most beautiful of the girl dancers, the one with the most bewitching eyes, the one who danced with Chahansa—he was certain she had winked at him!

"O My Good Phufadia," he whispered to himself. "If only you were here to taste these wonders!"

He thought once more of the kitchen and added, "There is more here to taste than you or I ever imagined!"

That night he slept in a soft bed in a room given him for his own. He was as happy as he had ever found himself because of a belly filled, this time with toothsome leftovers.

"Dear Phufadia," he groaned, "the Superus has ordered me to stay here a lifetime. I know that I have promised to take your ashes to the desert, and I swear I'll not forget you, but it will be hard to leave this place." Then he added hastily, "Of course I will find a way from here and seek out the barren thornbush. I will go in a day or two—as soon as I have had enough to eat."

Ranji fell asleep dreaming of the fragrance of the kitchen and of the eyes of the youngest and most beautiful of the girl dancers.

The next day went by, and the next. Ranji had no time to find a way from the palace of the Superus, for when he was not entertaining the Mighty One or talking with Chahansa or watching the youngest and most beautiful of the girl dancers, he was busy in the kitchen.

"Here comes our favorite taster," the cooks would call out. "He can taste more than anyone!"

He often met Chahansa in the kitchen, and they tasted together. They soon became close friends.

"I must not taste too much," Chahansa confided. "For if I grow fat, I'll not be able to dance, and I love to dance more than anything in my life."

"Mmm," Ranji nodded, his mouth full. "I dance some, but not like you. I would rather taste than dance."

Chahansa always left the kitchen early because he had to practice his dancing. Ranji always left late.

"Forgive me, Phufadia, for not yet going to the desert," the youth would say when he went to bed at night. "It is hard to leave a good friend." And then he would fall asleep remembering the eyes of the young girl dancer and the blissful flavor of the *dal* and curd he had enjoyed that evening.

One day he asked Chahansa about the girl dancer.

"She works very hard," Chahansa told him, "and dances very well. She has time for nothing else."

"Surely she must have time to taste," Ranji exclaimed.

"Oh, yes. But the food is taken to where the women dancers stay. They do not roam freely about the palace and fortress as we do. It is the same with the Superani. She is forever confined with the women who attend her."

"The Superani!" Ranji exclaimed. "I did not know there was a superani!"

"There is. I have heard that she is the most beautiful of the beautiful. But she is sad—indeed, the unhappiest of superanis."

"Why? Tell me about her!" Ranji said eagerly.

"She and the Superus were married when they were very young, as is the custom," Chahansa told him. "She was only seven years old, and he was ten. The Superus at once had her locked away and has not seen her since. It has been almost twenty years now."

"Why did he lock her away?"

"Who can say? Perhaps he did not like her. Now, of course, he is too fat to want a wife anyway. But they say—" Chahansa stopped suddenly.

"What do they say?" Ranji asked.

"Never mind," Chahansa said. "I don't like gossip. Here! Let us walk along the far side of the palace. I will show you the window where the Superani is allowed to sit and look out upon the world."

Ranji wanted to know what the gossip was and

promised himself he would find out. And so that very noon when he went to taste, he asked the fourth cook's apprentice, "What foods are carried to the Superani?"

"Whatever she wants, but it is never very much. Her ladies say she has little appetite because the years go by and the end of her life draws nearer."

"So it is for all of us," Ranji said philosophically as he popped a bite of *seekh kabab* into his mouth.

"Ah, but it is shorter for the Superani, for if she does not soon bear a son, the Superus will have her hanged."

"But . . . !" Ranji exclaimed.

"True! How can she bear a son if there is no father? Alas, the lady is in a situation of great difficulty!"

"That is not fair!" Ranji protested.

"Not at all," agreed the assistant and began mincing a clove of garlic.

Ranji was sorry to hear this and ate twice as much as he usually did.

That same afternoon the Superus asked him to twine his arms and legs like four tendrils of a grapevine. Ranji found himself wound so tightly he could scarcely unwind himself. The Superus was amused but fortunately did not laugh aloud.

When he had untangled himself, the boy loosened his belt. I am growing fat from all the tasting, he thought. I will soon be unable to tangle and untangle myself! He was worried enough about himself that he forgot about the gossip.

He confided his worry to Chahansa.

"You must stop tasting so much," Chahansa warned him.

"I can't!" Ranji groaned, and racked his brains for new tricks that would keep the Superus from asking him to put his knees behind his ears and his chin on his toes. He also began watching anxiously for any sign of displeasure the Mighty One might show. The boy came to know each twitch of mouth and droop of eye on that glum face.

"Oh, Phufadia," he whispered one night. "Do not let him hang me just because I like to taste!"

6

A Day Gone Wrong

One morning Ranji woke with not a single new idea in his head.

"Perhaps a good breakfast will help me think of something," he told himself, "otherwise I shall have to use the ones I have saved. Once they are gone, I shall have to leave here." And off he hurried.

But when Ranji came to the kitchen, he noticed that everything seemed to be going wrong. The first cook burned his tongue while tasting the cold cucumber soup. The second cook cut off the tip of his finger with a wooden ladle. The third cook watched a kettle so closely, it would not boil. The fourth cook's hand trembled so much that the coriander pods leaped from it like frightened chicks from a basket. The fifth cook wept because he had rubbed his eyes after cutting up hot peppers. The sixth cook brought down his cleaver and, missing the chopping board, almost lost a toe when the cleaver flew from his hand, shaved off the side of his sandal, and stood quivering at the edge of his foot, the blade fast in the floor.

So it went for all twenty of the cooks, and the twenty apprentices as well.

"What is the matter?" Ranji asked.

"Alas!" the first cook's apprentice cried with no grin at all on his round face. "We are all nervous because today someone will be chosen to be hanged."

"Why will that be?" Ranji asked, sipping at a spoonful of tasteless broth. He wrinkled his nose. "I have heard of no crime that was committed."

"Oh, this hanging is no punishment," the fifth cook told him. "It is merely the custom. It started long ago, when people were inclined to steal and kill for a living. For that, many were hanged every day. By the time the stealing and killing had stopped, hanging had become the custom, so it had to be continued. At first there was one each day."

"Then only one each a week."

"The father of the Superus had one hanged only once a month."

"Now it happens only once a year."

"And today is the day the person will be chosen."

"Tomorrow he will be hanged."

"It is always worrisome for all of us until someone is chosen."

"Then it is worrisome only for the one who was chosen."

"What is almost as worrisome to us is that the Superus wants twice as much to eat after the hanging, so we have to create eight hundred instead of four hundred dishes." The seventh cook gnawed at his thumbnail.

"But who will be hanged?" Ranji asked.

"Aaiii," said the fourteenth cook, "if we knew that, we would be singing while we cooked. But none in the whole fortress knows who it is the Superus will choose."

"It might be me, it might be you," the ninth cook said, and wiped away a tear.

Hearing those words, Ranji put down the fork without even sniffing at the morsel on the end of it. Surely it was time to continue his journey.

Ranji did not wait for Chahansa to come for his breakfast but hurried at once to his room and filled his sack with what tricks he had—those and the jar of ashes.

"It is time, Phufadia," he murmured. "I will put your dear ashes to rest."

"What about Chahansa?" The voice was Phufadia's. Ranji had not heard it in some time and was so startled that he almost dropped his sack. He looked around quickly. Of course the old faquir was not there.

"I will find Chahansa and we shall go together," Ranji cried, ashamed that he had not thought sooner of his friend.

He searched and searched everywhere for Chahansa but could not find him. At last, sorry to the depths of his heart, he hurried out of the palace and through the streets of the fortress toward the great gates.

"Forgive me, my friend," he whispered. "I have come to the end of my tricks and I do not wish to hang. But you who dance so beautifully—you surely will never hang!"

So comforting himself, he came to the gates. There he was stopped.

"Where do you think *you* are going?" asked the tallest of the eleven guards, made even taller by the cream-colored turban wound around his head.

"I feel that the Superus has seen enough of me and my tricks," Ranji said lightly. "It is time someone new entertained him. Besides, I have a sacred duty to perform, and so I am taking my leave."

"Ah, no," said the guard. "This day no one leaves except at the word of the Superus. We have had no word from him. He must think you have yet at least one new trick for him."

"I do not want to disappoint him," Ranji argued.

"He will let you know when you disappoint him," said the guard with a wide grin, and the other ten guards lined up behind him with their hands on the hilts of their shining curved swords. They too grinned at him.

Ranji pressed his palms together, bowed his head, and turned back. If there was any other way out of the fortress, he did not know it, for he had always been too busy tasting to hunt for one. Back he went to his room.

There he found Chahansa waiting for him.

"I did not see you at breakfast," Chahansa said.

"I left early," Ranji told him. "I looked for you but did not find you. I was strolling about the fortress. I need new ideas."

This was true, but not quite the whole truth, and shame again flooded through Ranji that he should say this to his friend.

But Chahansa merely nodded. "We all need something new, today especially. I was practicing all morning."

Ranji bowed his head to hide his burning face.

That afternoon Ranji and Chahansa sat side by side as they waited to perform. They had nothing to say to each other until Chahansa whispered, "May it not be you."

"May it not be you either," Ranji whispered in return, and watched as his friend joined the dancers and musicians. Though he was certain no harm would come to his friend, he could not help but worry about Chahansa, so he slipped aside to where he might watch both the dancers and the face of the Superus, every expression of which he knew so well.

All of the dancers were dancing their very best, and his friend had never danced so well. How he leaped! How he twirled! Surely it would not be possible for the Superus to choose him!

But as he watched the Superus, he could see that the Mighty One was not pleased. He frowned and scowled, his brow growing blacker by the moment.

He grumbled and muttered and scratched his thigh, for he could not reach his chin across the bulge of his belly.

When the dancing had finished, there was silence in the room. No one dared speak until the Superus had formed a judgment.

At last, his eyes fierce and angry, the Superus raised his hand and pointed.

"That one," he said. "That one must be hanged tomorrow."

And he pointed at Chahansa.

The youngest and most beautiful of the girl dancers cried out.

"No! No! Not Chahansa! For I love him!" and she threw herself at the feet of the Superus.

Luckily the Superus could not peer over his belly to see which dancer lay at his feet, or the youngest and most beautiful of the girl dancers might also have hanged. For if the Superus could change the custom from one hanging each month to one hanging each year, might he not start a new custom with two hangings each year? The other dancers gathered around her quickly and carried her from the room while thirteen guards seized Chahansa and led him away to prison, where he would await hanging the next day.

Ranji was stunned.

Not only had he lost his friend, but the youngest and most beautiful of the dancers, who, he was certain, had always had eyes only for him, really loved Chahansa!

And then the most terrible thought came to his mind.

If Chahansa were gone, perhaps she would come to love him, Ranji.

So horrified by this thought that he could not bear to examine it, Ranji rushed from the room.

Fortunately for him, the Superus declared at that same instant, "There will be no more amusement for today. I shall save myself for watching the hanging tomorrow."

Ranji hurried to his own room. He threw himself to his knees, bowed to the floor, covered his head with his hands, and moaned. Surely something evil had grown in him to give him such a thought! Besides that, "I made three promises!" he sobbed. "I vowed to carry the ashes of my beloved Phufadia to the desert. I vowed to help the starving villagers. I vowed eternal friendship to Chahansa! But what have I done? I have neglected everything to eat myself as fat as a rooting pig!

"Is this what comes of a full stomach? That I would wish my friend to die? That I would become so fat, I could not perform my tricks? That I would forget about the hunger in the village and eat with no remorse from the labor of their hands while they starved? That I would leave the ashes of my beloved Phufadia to stand in a jar in the corner, waiting and waiting?"

He crouched, covering his face with his hands, rocking back and forth and weeping. "What is there of me that is worthy of anything? Why cannot I be hanged in place of my friend, who wanted only to dance so beautifully that he would make people weep for joy?"

"Ah, a full belly and an empty heart," said a voice that Ranji recognized at once. It was that of Phufadia.

"O My Dear Phufadia!" His agony was so great that these were the only words Ranji could choke out.

"Well, you are forgiven," said the voice after a moment. "For you are truly sorry. Besides, have you forgotten that you are a scamp and an imp and full of mischief?"

"What good is that?" the boy sobbed without looking up.

"You have had nothing to eat today" came Phufadia's gentle voice. "Perhaps you will have a vision."

Ranji sniffed, wiped his eyes on his sleeve, and straightened his back. "It would take a week of fasting to bring a vision," he said. "Perhaps a month. Perhaps a year, I have eaten so much!"

"Perhaps you will have a dream."

"I dream of nothing but tasting and the eyes of the most beautiful girl dancer," wailed Ranji.

"Then perhaps you will at least have an idea."

"To keep him from asking me to put my legs behind my ears and my chin on my feet, all my ideas have gone to invent new tricks for the Superus—just so I could keep stuffing myself," Ranji mourned. "I don't know if I *could* have a different kind of thought. I only wish I could die for my friend."

As Phufadia's voice did not reply to this, Ranji sat on the floor with his legs crossed, his forefingers and thumbs touching. He closed his eyes and bowed his head.

But neither vision nor dream came, nor even an idea other than that he longed to die for his friend. For his mind would not be still enough to let in a different idea. One minute it was filled with anguish, the next it hopped from one memory to another, all of them old and of no use at all to Chahansa.

Ranji sat still for so long that at last his eyes did not know they were closed. His head nodded forward.

7

A Short Chapter of Dreams, Visions, and One Idea

It was all wrong, of course, as such dreams always are. Ranji found himself mourning for Chahansa as he walked through the country with the Superus riding beside him on a water buffalo.

"When we reach the thornbush, you will hang the water buffalo from the highest branch," the Superus told the boy.

"Then what will you ride on, O Mighty Superus?"

"You will carry me on your back or I will hang *you*," growled the Superus.

Ranji reached up and drew a rabbit from the knee of the Superus. "This is your soul," he told the Mighty One. "It will be much easier to hang a hare than a buffalo, and you will still be able to ride the bullock."

"Hang my soul!" roared the Superus. "What do you take me for?"

Before Ranji could answer, the bullock spoke in the voice of Phufadia. "Boys whose minds have turned to burnt sugar pudding are not allowed to hang rabbits. They must fast."

"But with too much fasting the children of the village starve and die," Ranji protested.

"Who will die?" the Superus asked anxiously. Then he cried, "You, of course! I will have you hanged! Now I must have my dinner! Hoo! Get on there!" He kicked his heels into the sides of the water buffalo, and the creature galloped away.

"Ranji! Ranji!"

Startled, the boy turned around. He now stood in his own room. There, in the moonlight that lay in silver patterns across the floor, crouched an old woman. She was dressed in rags more tattered than any he had ever seen. When she raised her head he saw a pinch-lipped hag whose face wrinkled in a thousand creases. She leaned toward him.

"Ranji," she croaked, "am I not beautiful?"

The boy's mouth dropped open. He could not think quickly enough to answer her before she cackled. "Oh, but I am!" she cried. "I am the most beautiful woman you have ever seen!"

Then, with a quick movement of her hand, she tugged at her face and pulled away a mask.

There was the face of the beautiful grandmother he had twice dreamed of.

"Ranji!" she murmured. "Use your wits! Empty your bowl of rice and fill it with mischief!"

Then she vanished.

With that, Ranji woke with a start. He was sitting on the mat, his legs folded, his nose in his lap. All of this had been a dream. Or was it a vision? What did it matter? The important thing was that Chahansa had not yet been hanged! Surely there was something in the dream that revealed how he might be saved.

Ranji sat up and held his head in his hands. *Use your wits!* But what would his wits tell him? He rocked back and forth on the mat trying desperately to think—not of a new story or a new trick, but of a way to save his friend.

In despair he bowed his head.

"Oh, Phufadia, how I wish I could remember something you told me that would help my friend. He loves so to dance and everyone loves to watch him. The pleasure he has given is more than what I can give. He was happy. And now he is to be hanged. No one knows why. And then I will be hanged too, because I will soon have no more tricks."

He sighed. "At least here I have always had more than enough to eat. Even so, I have never been as happy as I was with you. O Ashes of My Dear Phufadia, how patient you have been!" Again he covered his face with his hands.

"Yes, both Chahansa and I have had happy lives," he said into his palms, "though short ones."

Even as he spoke these brave words, tears crept through his fingers.

"And how much more fortunate we have been than the Superus!" he went on, sniffing, his breath catching. "He is so fat, he cannot walk. He cannot heave himself from his throne to look through the window at the blue sky. It takes seventeen men to carry him from his throne to his bed. He always wants to be amused, but he is scarcely ever amused and dares not even laugh. He has neither son nor daughter, for he has not seen his wife since she was seven years old, having locked her away where he cannot enjoy her company. He does not even know that she is beautiful!

"Poor Superani!" Ranji sobbed aloud. "He will have her hanged too, because she has given him no children. All he ever wants is more to eat. But his gluttony brings only heartburn and indigestion, bloating and wheezing. Never happiness."

This last was a truly new thought that came to Ranji, and he cried aloud, "Even though he receives everything he asks for, the Mighty Superus is not happy! He is miserable! Besides that, I do not doubt that he is afraid of dying!"

For a minute the boy sat still, his mouth hanging open. Then he leaped to his feet. "Of course!" he cried, and snapped his fingers. "Of course! Oh, thank you, thank you, dear old faquir! Thank you, beautiful grandmother! I'll do it!"

He rushed from his room.

8

Mischief

anji hurried through the palace, going first to the room where Chahansa had stayed. In half a minute he left, carrying a bundle under his arm. Next, though he had no right to go there, he crept through the shadows to the room where the youngest and most beautiful of the girl dancers stayed.

He found her not asleep but weeping. Touching his finger to his lips, he swore her to silence. Then he whispered into her ear words that made her gasp.

"But Ranji," she protested, "what if you are caught?"

"Then I shall die," he told her.

She burst into tears once more. "Then I shall have lost both of you!"

"No, no!" he said. "For Chahansa would go free. I should take his place. But do not worry. I will not be caught, and Chahansa will go free besides. I promise you!"

Her tears stopped at once, and in two minutes more he left her almost smiling.

Ranji too was almost smiling. Was it possible that she loved him too, just a little? What a beautiful girl she was! And wealthy as well! For had not Phufadia said that true wealth was love, and the more one loved, the richer one was? He hummed as he hurried to the room where the clothes were made for the Superus. He roused the best of the seamstresses and argued with her for seven minutes. At last she nodded.

"Yes," she said. "For, as you say, how do I know but that next year he may choose *me* to be hanged? And if this other is a way, perhaps it will become a custom." She took the bundle from him and lent him a pair of scissors.

From there Ranji went to the kitchen where the cooks were busy preparing for the next day's eight hundred meals. He argued with all twenty of the cooks and all twenty of the apprentices for seventeen minutes, until finally the twentieth cook nodded.

"Yes," he said. "For, as you say, how do we know but that each year for the next forty years he may choose one of *us* to be hanged? And if this other is a way, perhaps it will become a custom."

Ranji left the kitchen with a bowl of flour and a jug of water. He hastened to his room, where, without arguing a single moment with the straw mat upon the floor, he cut it to shreds and set to work. It was a good thing he did not pass time arguing with the mat, for the night was rushing through itself, and he had little time left.

It was scarcely two hours before dawn when he again hurried to the sleepy seamstress and, after kissing her on the cheek, rushed off—again with his arms full—to the prison where Chahansa was guarded by seven tall prison guards. They were all dressed in crimson and blue and had shining curved swords held at their sides by golden sashes. Their turbans were high and their beards curled under their chins.

There he argued for twenty-three minutes. He talked and he pleaded and he flung out his arms and danced up and down and flopped his head from side to side, until at last all seven nodded soberly.

"Yes," they said all in one breath. "For, as you say, how do we know but that for each of the next seven years he may not choose one of *us* to be hanged? And if this other is a way, perhaps it will become a custom."

Ranji was given entrance to the prison room, where he roused Chahansa and spoke quickly to him.

"But supposing that *you* are hanged for this?" Chahansa argued.

"No matter," Ranji said. "I have made three vows, and I must be true to them. You must do this to help me, or I will die of sorrow before I am hanged. Now hurry."

Three minutes later Ranji, empty-handed but not alone, left the cell.

The next stop was the gate of the fortress. There Ranji argued for thirty-nine minutes with the eleven tall gate guards.

Finally, just as the sun sent its first shining ray to touch the tip of the highest red-brick tower of the fortress of the Mighty Most Excellent Superus, eleven tall guards dressed in purple vests and green trousers, their heads wrapped in amber-colored turbans, eyed each other and, nodding, agreed.

"Yes," they said. "For, as you say, how do we know but that for each of the next eleven years he may not choose one of *us* to be hanged? And if this other is a way, perhaps it will become a custom."

The gate was opened and a lithe figure ran down the hill.

"Remember my message," Ranji called after the runner, "for it concerns the second vow I have made!"

* * *

Late that morning, just before the Superus had his lunch of eight hundred dishes, there was a hanging. Everyone in the palace was ordered to watch. The seventeen carriers of the Superus bore his Mighty Excellency to the window so that he too might watch.

"What a coward!" snorted the Superus. "They had to drag him to the gibbet and hold him up while they placed the noose around his neck. I was not amused by that dancer. He had no spirit."

Then the Mighty Most Excellent Superus scowled and grumbled his way through his lunch of eight hundred dishes. Immediately after the lunch, he demanded that Ranji come to him.

"I want to be amused," he growled. "I want to laugh

almost but not quite. Tell me a funny story, though not too funny."

Ranji wrung his hands together. Tears came to his eyes.

"O Mighty Superus," he said, "I have stories I could tell you that would almost make you laugh. But I cannot tell them to you."

"Must I have two hangings in one day?" the Superus roared. "Must I start a new custom? Why can't you tell them to me?"

"Ah, your Most High and Mighty, Most Excellent, Most Wondrous of All Possible Superuses, it is only this," Ranji began. "I have heard that a fabled old woman has come to this country—to this very fortress. My own ears have heard of her from before the time I was born. There is no one her equal at telling stories. She holds her listeners so spellbound the earth itself might vanish and they would never notice. How can I tell my own feeble tales when I know such a one is at hand?"

"I will have her brought to me," said the Superus. "Maybe I am growing weary of you. If I like her stories better than yours, I will have you hanged for my pleasure and have her tell me stories until I weary of her."

"You may not want her to come," Ranji said. "For she is also a teller of the future. And the future is not always kind!"

"Why should that bother me?" the Superus shouted, glaring at Ranji. "My future is as solid as my throne.

You will be hanged within the hour for such presumption! Call the guards!"

Ranji threw himself to his knees and touched his nose to the floor. "As you wish, O Mighty Superus!" he cried, and said to himself, I was right, my dear Phufadia. Then, as he was led from the room, he called over his shoulder, "I wish you long life and good health, O Most Excellent Superus. May you enjoy forever the stories of the old woman. You will find her easily. You have only to ask for her by name."

"Wait!" shouted the Superus. "What is her name?"

Ranji put his fingers to his lips and thought for some moments. "Alas," he said. "The thought of being hanged has made me forget it. But I would know her in a moment, for I saw her once when I was very young. Farewell, O Mightiest of Superuses."

"Wait!" shouted the Superus. "You must bring her to me. I will not have you hanged until tomorrow! Go and find her."

Ranji bowed. "I shall search every corner of the fortress. When I have found her, I will send her to you."

"I want her this very evening," growled the Superus.

"You shall have her if she still breathes the air of this world," Ranji said, and hurried so quickly from the throne room of the Mighty Superus that the guards were left behind.

9

Ijnarini

That very evening an old woman appeared at the palace of the Highest Most Excellent Superus. She was stooped and walked with the help of a cane. She wore a tattered dress and a much patched gray cloak with a hood that modestly covered her face.

"I am Ijnarini, the storyteller," she quavered in an old and shaky voice. "Ranji, the quick of hand and tongue, tells me that the Superus bid me come."

She was hurried to the Superus, who was chewing his underlip when he was not gnawing a bone held in the fingers of one of his feeders, for he was impatient for amusement, having had none since the hanging.

"O Mighty Superus," the old woman said. "It is my understanding that your greatest of delights rests in a good tale well told. I will tell you such a tale in the best way I know how. There was once a kingdom in which dwelt a wonderful golden bird." She began her story in the same breath, never giving the Superus a chance to say a word. "This bird lived on a particular kind of thistle seed which grew only in the King's garden, and so it stayed there at all times, taking its fill of thistle seeds and singing its songs.

"The songs it sang were so beautiful that no one could hold back tears on hearing them. Not only that, but when the notes of the songs flew forth into the air, they turned to pearls and diamonds and dropped to the ground in a shower. It was indeed a marvelous bird, and the King loved it dearly.

"Every day, after it sang, the King wiped away his tears of joy and gathered the jewels that had fallen from the lovely notes.

"Now the King was a good king and a happy king, for he was a loving king. He loved his bird not just for the jewels. He loved it for its beauty and the beauty of its songs. He also loved his people. He invited the poor of his country into his garden to hear the lovely songs. Then he gave them all of the song-jewels, as they were called, so that the people too might have everything that would make them happy.

"For this the bird loved the King, because love begets love. Each morning at dawn it began its songs for him and sang until dusk. So many jewels fell from the ravishing notes that soon there were no poor left in the country. Because of this the people loved the King. The country was one great circle of love enfolding people, King, and bird, and so it was the wealthiest country in the world.

"But though there were no poor, there were those who were greedy. For greed has nothing to do with poverty or wealth. It is an illness. Alas, that there are so many who suffer from this affliction! But suffer they do, and the suffering is that they think they must always have more than they need.

"Thus it happened that because of greed, the King woke one day and did not hear the bird singing.

" 'Where is my bird?' he cried.

"The palace and the palace garden were searched from one end to the other. Each nook, each cranny, of the palace was looked into. Every leaf of each tree and shrub was parted from the next, but no trace of the bird was found, not even a single golden feather.

"The King mourned. The people of the palace mourned. The word soon traveled throughout the country, and all the people of the country mourned. Everyone searched and hunted everywhere, but no one found the precious bird.

"What the King and all of his court and all of his people but one did not know was that the bird had been stolen by the greediest rogue in the land. He was one who always had all he needed but never found that enough. He wanted everything in the world for himself. And so, of course, he wanted the bird.

"One night he entered the palace garden—there were no guards, for what need was there for guards when there was no need for theft?—climbed the tree where the bird slept, seized it by the neck, put it into a sack, and thrust it into a rusty cage. He then carried it off to the mountains, where there was a cave high on the side of a cliff that no one but himself knew of. In that dark cave he hid the bird. The next morning he waited for it to sing.

"But the bird was used to beginning its song when the first light of day appeared, so how could it sing in a darkness where the sun never dawned? It remained silent.

"Now this brigand, this thief, was clever, but he was also a cruel man. After waiting three days for the bird to sing, he decided that the jewels must lie in the bird's throat, whence came its song. He would cut its throat and take the precious stones. Then, as the bird would be of no further use to him, he would roast it for his dinner.

"He gathered sticks and built a fire. Then he opened the door of the cage and reached—"

Suddenly the old woman stopped her words, moaned, and put her hands to her face.

"What is it?" asked the Superus, and then commanded, "Continue with your story. I must hear the end of it or I will have you hanged!"

Much agitated, Ijnarini rocked back and forth. "I cannot tell you, for I have had a vision that concerns you."

"Tell me your vision and then continue the story!" ordered the Superus.

"No one else must hear what my vision showed me," moaned the old woman.

"Then whisper it in my ear!" he demanded.

Ijnarini came as close as she could to the Superus's ear, cupped her hand about her mouth, and whispered.

"O Mighty Superus! My vision comes from Shamshana-Kali, and it is this. For three hundred days you must live like the peasants of the village below the fortress, or you will die tomorrow. You must make up your mind at once which you prefer."

The Superus was so startled, he could not answer. The old woman went on. "If you choose to die, preparations must be made this very moment for your funeral. You can plan them yourself. Why don't you—"

"No! No!" cried the Superus. "I choose to live!"

"Then it must be like a peasant," said Ijnarini. "Call for the boy Ranji. He has seen how they live. He must be the only one to serve you." Then she clasped her hands and shook her head. "But it may be too late, for you ordered him to be hanged!"

"Not until tomorrow!" said the Superus in a voice that now trembled more than that of the old woman.

"Thank the gods for that!" cried Ijnarini. "For in the next three hundred days you must lay eyes on no other in the palace! Nor must any other lay eyes on you! The boy Ranji must take care of all your needs and carry your orders to those beyond your door. I shall go and call him at once!"

With that, she rushed from the room.

"Stop her! Catch her!" roared the Superus, finding his loudest voice. "And then bring that imp and scamp of a Ranji to me!"

The frightened guards chased after the woman. But she had vanished as quickly as Ranji had earlier in the day, and search as they would, they could find neither trick nor turn of either of them. The guards had not the least idea in which corner to search. They rushed here and there and everywhere, their curved swords knocking at their knees. Then suddenly, in the hallway just outside the Superus's throne room, there came Ranji, a smile on his face.

"Ijnarini has told me that the Superus needs me," he said. "I am at his service."

Happy to have at least one of them, the guards seized the boy and hurried him into the throne room.

"And where is Ijnarini?" the Superus demanded to know.

The guards gnawed their knuckles and stared at the floor.

Ranji bowed low and came to their aid. "How can they know, O Mighty Superus, when I myself do not know? For I understand that I was the last one to see her when she came running to tell me I must come to you. It was a hard thing for such an old woman to run so fast! I knew it was a matter of great urgency and I came quickly. As for Ijnarini, she was before me one minute and had vanished the next. It is a way she has. But she gave me a message for you."

"What is that?" snarled the Superus.

"I do not understand what she meant by it, O Mighty One, but I shall give you her exact words."

The boy, clearly thinking hard, touched his fingertips together and brought them to his lips. He closed his eyes. The Superus fidgeted.

At last Ranji spoke. "She said, 'Tell his Excellency, the Highest and Most Mighty Superus, that when the three hundred days have been accomplished, I will return and finish the story. Otherwise, as he knows, all stories will be finished for him tomorrow at the first ray of the sun, or on any day of the three hundred days that he breaks his chosen way of living.' Then she said, 'You, Ranji, will serve the Superus as he demands you serve him.' "

Ranji bowed and added, "With those words, she was gone. What did she mean, O Mighty Superus? Since I came here I have always served you the best I know how. How can I serve you further?"

"Aaargh!" shrieked the Superus, and beat his hands against his thighs. "She has brought word to me from the very mouth of Shamshana-Kali!"

"Ahhh!" The breath left Ranji.

"Ahhh!" The breath left the lungs of all others in the throne room.

"That is serious indeed!" Ranji whispered just loud enough for all to hear, and shook his head gravely.

Then "Out!" shouted the Superus to the guards and ministers and all other servants who stood stunned and wordless before him. "All of you! Out of my sight! You, Ranji! You alone will stay and serve me!"

10·

Preparations for the
Three Hundred Days

After he had been alone with the Excellent Superus for the breath of two moments, Ranji pressed his palms together and bowed his head.

"O Mighty Superus, now that you have told me of the vision of Ijnarini, we must take the greatest care that not a single second of tomorrow comes without your life being protected. Everything must be removed from this room at once to make it like the house of a peasant. That will take some time. As it is already late in the evening, we must first hide you, lest someone be here a second past midnight. I know you will be uncomfortable"—the greatest sympathy sounded in the boy's voice—"and I beg you forgive me for what I must do."

"Do what you must do!" ordered the frightened Superus. "Do it quickly!"

Ranji then left the Superus alone and went to the best of the seamstresses.

"I must have the widest, longest, heaviest piece of cloth in your possession," he said.

Knowing that Ranji had reason, she searched through her pieces of cloth. It so happened that she had one designed to cover the largest of the royal elephants.

Scarcely able to drag it behind him it was so heavy, Ranji hurried the best he could back to the throne room. The boy then draped the cloth over the head and shoulders and as much of the belly of the Superus as it would cover.

"There," he said with satisfaction. "You can see no one and no one can see you. You will be safe even today!"

"It's stuffy" came the muffled grumble of the Superus.

"Not as stuffy as a tomb," the boy reminded him.

At the shuddering of the Mighty Superus, the heavy drape rippled like a lake before a storm.

Now Ranji called all of the servants. "By order of the Mighty Superus, every trace of elegance in this throne room must be removed. It must be left empty by one minute before midnight," he told them.

All of the palace servants swarmed into the room. With Ranji directing them, they emptied the pool of sapphires. The coffers of rubies and basins of emeralds were carried away. Agate, pearl, and carnelian were dug from the walls until it was a room bare of all ornament, much like the rest of the palace.

"You must place a stone bench against the wall beside the throne," Ranji ordered.

This was done.

"You cannot have a throne to sit upon, or have the seventeen men carry you to your soft bed," Ranji whispered to the Superus. "It would not be the way of the peasants." Ranji then unrolled a straw mat upon the bench, and the draped figure of the Superus was lifted to it by the seventeen men.

Then even the marble throne of the Eminent Superus was dragged off. As this was done, the boy's eyes widened, for there, behind where the throne had stood, was a door. The back door to the palace. The back door to the very fortress, for the back wall of the palace and the fortress were one.

Ranji clasped his hands together and closed his eyes. His mind turned in such a loop, it left him dizzy. I could take the ashes of Phufadia and run away this very night, he thought. Then he bit his lip. Or I could use the door for another purpose, he told himself humbly.

"Place the table outside that door," he ordered, and last of all went the great table that had so lately borne the weight of eight hundred separate dishes of the most delicious comestibles in the world.

At one minute to midnight the weary servants departed from a room now totally bare.

Ranji took away the cloth that had swathed the Superus.

"You are safe now. Let me help you," he murmured, and with the greatest effort managed to tip the Mighty

One to his side so that he could sleep on the stone bench.

Ranji spread a mat for himself upon the floor and lay down upon it.

"Oh, Phufadia," he whispered to himself as the tired Superus began to snore. "I am not sure which of us will have the greatest penance. I know that it will be hard to serve the Superus. But I have made three vows. The third, which I saw to first, was to save the life of Chahansa. The Superus does not know that a puppet with the likeness of my friend's face hangs from the gibbet and that for three hundred days Chahansa will entertain the people of the village with his dancing.

"The people of the village! My second promise was to them. But will I live to help them? The door—I *could* take your ashes tonight, my dear Phufadia, and at least fulfill my promise to you."

Ranji sat up and stared for a long time at the door. At last, with a sigh, he lay down again. "No, I must stay to do all I can for the villagers. *Last,* my beloved faquir, will be my promise to your ashes. I hope I live to carry them to the great desert."

Then, though his belly was empty, for he had been too busy that night to do any tasting, he murmured, "I fear I have emptied the rice from my bowl. I hope the mischief I fill it with will serve everyone."

The boy yawned, then fell asleep and slept soundly because, whatever the state of his bowl, his heart was comfortable.

* * *

The next morning, before dawn, Ranji visited the kitchen.

"I have orders from the Mighty Superus that you are to cook the usual four hundred dishes for each meal," he said. "There is this difference. There will not be three but only two such meals prepared each day. Morning and evening. All of the dishes are to be set in a row outside the wall of the fortress at the back of the palace behind the throne room. Then everyone must leave. Under punishment of death, no one is to look upon that place except when the dishes are brought there and again when you take them away. I myself will serve the Superus his meals, which I shall bring him through the door in the farthest wall of the palace. I shall return the empty dishes to the same place, and you will return to remove them when you are called.

"There is yet another thing. Twice a day you will also bring a bowl containing exactly thirty-seven grains of rice, and . . ." Ranji finished giving his order. The cooks shook their heads at the strangeness of it all.

Next he gave orders to all others who dwelt in palace and fortress. For the next three hundred days they were to continue in all their duties just as they had when the Superus received them in his throne room. There was one exception. No one from the fortress, not guard nor minister nor stable boy, under punishment of death, was ever to look behind the wall at the back of the throne room.

However . . . there was one last pronouncement.

"The Mighty Superus orders that word be carried to the people of the village at the foot of the hill. They must climb the hill twice a day, morning and evening, and circle the fortress once. They must cry out a blessing of thanks for the generosity and courage of his Insuperable Majesty. Only they are allowed to pass behind the throne room, for the Greatest of All Great Ones wishes to hear their voices clearly."

After that, Ranji hurried to speak briefly with the youngest and most beautiful of the girl dancers.

"You too will go to the village at the foot of the hill below the fortress," he told her. "You will bring word that each time they come to the back wall of the palace to cry their thanks, they must serve themselves from the dishes they find there. Whatever they cannot eat, they must leave. After that they will march back to their village. They must tell no one from the palace that they have dined. This they will do for three hundred days. It is so ordered by the Mighty Superus himself. It is also ordered that you tell no one in the palace of this."

Then Ranji smiled at the youngest and most beautiful of the dancers. "You must bring this order to the dancer who is to stay in the house of the blind woman of the village until the Superus asks for his return. It is also ordered that you breathe no word of this to any other."

With a cry of joy, the youngest and most beautiful of the dancers blew Ranji a kiss and took her way quickly from the palace.

Ranji sighed deeply and wiped the stinging from his eyes. "What must be must be," he murmured sadly, and returned to the Superus.

* * *

It was with much groaning and puffing and snorting from both Ranji and the Superus that the Mighty One was at last set upright and made ready for his breakfast.

"I hurt all over from that bed of stone," growled the Superus.

"It will not always hurt so much, for you will get as used to it as the peasants are to the hard ground," Ranji said. "Then you will truly be living like a peasant."

"I am still alive, so I must already be living like a peasant," snapped the Superus. "Where is my breakfast?"

"It is here. A peasant's breakfast," Ranji announced cheerfully. "Thirty-seven grains of rice and a cup of whey in the morning."

"What about lunch?"

"No lunch."

The Superus's eyes opened in alarm. "And dinner?"

"A bowl of thirty-seven grains of rice in the evening. Every fifth day the head and tail of a boiled fish will be added to the rice. Every seventeenth day a burned carrot will come with it. On the twenty-ninth day of each month you will be served with your rice a piece of goat cheese the size of my thumb. Water you will have—all you want, though it may be slightly brackish."

The Superus sniffed at the air.

"But I can smell the four hundred different aromas of my usual breakfast!" he complained.

"True," Ranji agreed. "You see, the peasants of the village at the bottom of the hill can smell the kitchen of the Mighty Superus all day every day, for the wind bears the wondrous aromas to them as they go to and come from the fields where they work. So it is that you must live as they do."

The Superus groaned and bowed his head.

After a while Ranji fed him the thirty-seven grains of rice, one at a time.

11

The First Hundred Days

Every day there wafted into the room the mouth-watering redolence of multitudinous dishes spiced with cloves and cinnamon, nutmeg and cardamom, onions and mangoes, cumin and peppers, ginger and fenugreek, garlic and coriander.

"Remember that the village of the peasants lies downwind from the palace," Ranji again explained to the Superus. "The breezes that come to them bear the delicious emanations from the kitchen. I am sure it makes them happy to be able to have such fragrances come to their noses as they eat their thirty-seven grains of rice. I beg you, breathe deeply, so that you will be equally happy and truly living like a peasant."

The Superus beat his fists against his thighs and pulled his lips sidewise into a grimace that he hoped would pass for a smile.

"Oh yes, I am happy!" he said. "These are tears of joy that run down my face."

"Good," Ranji said. "Your joy keeps you alive."

So every day everything was prepared as usual for

the Superus, as well as the bowl of thirty-seven grains of rice and the glass of whey that Ranji had requested for himself. Within the fortress the cooks remarked upon the odd change of taste of the youth in asking now and then for a single burned carrot or the boiled head and tail of a fish or an occasional piece of goat cheese, and wondered if this was some form of cleansing that he had taken upon himself. Ranji never explained, and the diet did not vary for a hundred days.

Outside, each day, morning and night, the villagers circled the fortress and, all with their spoons, cried a blessing of thanks for the courage of the Superus. Then they took bites from as many as they could of the four hundred dishes of food prepared for the Mighty One. Again, when they had finished their meal, they cried a blessing of thanks to him for his bounty. After they left, Ranji tasted three of the dishes himself and then sent for the servants.

He was careful not to overeat, lest he grow fat before the eyes of the Superus. He partook only of plain rice and a few bites of fresh fruit and vegetables, so that the scent of herbs and spices might not be left on his breath. But his mouth watered over the mounds of delicious foods he knew would be polished off by all who dwelt in the fortress.

"Oh, my dear Phufadia!" he would murmur, his eyes tearing as he watched the savory dishes taken off, the plates and bowls and platters to be emptied, washed, and filled again with the delicacies the cooks still prepared night and day for the Superus.

It appeared to the cooks and carriers of the leftover food that about the same amount as usual was being devoured by the Superus. For he had indeed consumed as much as two dozen peasants could manage at each meal. Though he was making do without his noon meal, no one thought to wonder if the Superus might be hungry.

Through the rest of the day Ranji kept himself busy, though his tasks were not the easiest to bear. For the Superus, once he had been fed his thirty-seven grains of rice, was not an easy man to live with.

He was hungry every minute of the day and night. His belly growled and howled and roared and snorted. The Mighty One was certain that there dwelt within his middle parts two little men. One little man stamped and twisted and turned grotesque somersaults, while the other forever prodded his insides with an iron poker heated to a glowing red, so that those middle parts burned and twisted and turned. They cramped so painfully, they caused the Superus to weep. Such waterfalls of tears ran down his cheeks and over his monstrous paunch to the floor that it was like the salt sea coming from the eyes of a whale and falling over the edges of the earth.

"It is from joy! From joy!" he would reassure Ranji, and then he himself would growl and howl and roar even more loudly than his belly, which convinced the servants and guards and ministers of the palace that all was well with him, for did they not hear his voice every day?

"I am singing!" he would explain to Ranji. "Is this not how the peasants sing? It is the best I can do!"

"They could do no better than you!" Ranji assured him.

Often the Superus sighed. "If only I might be distracted from my inner voices by an outer amusement, it would be easier to be a peasant. Do the peasants never have someone to amuse them?"

Ranji said, "Alas, the villagers cannot afford to pay for one to amuse them, and even if they offered to share their thirty-seven grains of rice with such a one, how could they then stay alive?"

The Superus sighed, and admitted it would be difficult to live on less than what they had. But one day the Mighty One was so mournful that Ranji could not bear to see him weep so. The boy clapped his hand to his head.

"I have just thought of something! The day before I came here, I myself provided the peasants of the village with an hour of entertainment. I would have charged them nothing, but they insisted I have a share in their dinner. Truly it should be permitted I give you the same!"

The Superus watched eagerly as Ranji did the simplest of his tricks and told the simplest of his stories, none of them new to the Mighty One—he had seen and heard them once before—but somehow they were fresh in the repeated performance.

"What a pleasure it is to watch you! There is much you do that I never noticed before, because I was so busy eating!" the Superus cried. And so delighted was he with all of it that he laughed aloud. Nor did he cough, for it was the middle of the afternoon and there was no crumb to come into his throat.

"A joy! A pleasure!" he repeated, and clapped his hands together.

"A joy, a pleasure to entertain you!" said Ranji with a bow.

That evening he took a share of the Superus's thirty-seven grains of rice. "I shall take only nine," Ranji told him. "Do not fear. I would do the same if I were sharing with a peasant."

The eyes of the Superus filled with tears that blurred the sight of the vanishing grains. He counted them as Ranji popped them one by one into his mouth.

Afterward Ranji smiled, rubbed his stomach, and remarked, "What a pleasant day this was!"

The Superus nodded mutely.

Whatever the Superus's true feelings, Ranji was pleased. Pleased because for a whole hour he had not had to listen to the whining complaints of the Mighty One; pleased even more with himself, for he had enjoyed his own tricks; pleased for yet another reason.

"O My Beloved Phufadia, who would guess at the mischief I am serving from my bowl?" he whispered in the night when the snores of the Superus were loud. "But I think that if you were here, you would not sigh and scold me. You would say it was a good thing."

Ranji then struck a spark to a candle and sheltered

it with his body so that the light would not waken the Superus. He went on whispering to the old faquir's ashes. "Because for the first time in the memory of the Superus being the Superus, the Mighty One was able to clap his hands together before his belly and laugh without strangling himself on his own breath!"

Ranji paused to lick the end of a thread and thrust it through the eye of a needle before continuing his one-sided conversation.

"The Highest One did not notice it because I was too busy distracting him. Besides, such a thought has not entered his mind. He has no mirror, and this task of mine has kept him from noticing what has been happening for some weeks." Ranji deftly caught up the seams of the Mighty One's shirt and trousers and then snipped away the extra cloth with a pair of scissors he had borrowed from the best of all the seamstresses.

"He does not notice because, alas, poor Superus, from each day to the next his clothes fit him as snugly as ever!" Ranji sighed, and then grinned the grin of an imp and a scamp, after which he bit off the end of the thread and blew out the candle.

* * *

But being a scamp and an imp was not always easy. For if the Superus was growing thinner with living on only seventy-four grains of rice a day and an occasional boiled fish head and tail and now and again a burned carrot, to say nothing of an exceedingly rare bite of goat cheese, there might come a time when the Highest Most Excellent One discovered it. He might be fearful at finding himself wasting away and become terrified that he would die of such a discomfort. Ranji prepared himself from minute to minute of each day. He fixed words in his mind so that he would have them ready to assure the Superus that he was living like a peasant and in that way prolonging his life.

Every minute of every day he must soothe the Highest Most Excellent One, who was forever disturbed at being so hungry. One day the agitation of the Superus was so great that, without noticing what he did, he pushed himself to his feet and staggered around his room, wringing his hands and beating his fists against his breast.

"There was never so miserable a peasant as myself!" he sobbed. "I am so hungry, I could eat the very pearls off the walls. But the jewels have all been taken away."

"You could not eat them if they were still there," Ranji assured him. "For even with the finest sauce, they have been found inedible. If you were a peasant of the village, you might eat grass with your goats, or dig up the root of a thornbush and try it, if that was all there was. Indeed, there is often nothing else for them. Not even thirty-seven grains of rice."

"Ah, if only I had some grass!" cried the Superus, sinking back onto his stone bench, still not realizing that he had been on his feet.

"I'll see what I can do," Ranji said soothingly.

The next day a mound of grass lay beside his bowl of rice. The Superus thrust a handful into his mouth. It was uncooked and stringy, hard to chew and even harder to swallow. Knowing he had partaken of what goats and donkeys ate, he did not feel well the rest of the day.

"Will I die of it?" he asked Ranji anxiously.

"The peasants don't die of eating grass," Ranji assured him.

"Ah, if only I had the root of a thornbush," the Superus mourned.

"I'll see what I can do," Ranji told him.

Three days later a twisted brown thong lay beside the Superus's dish of rice.

"What's that?" asked the Mighty One, who that morning had been looking forward to his burned carrot.

"The root of a thornbush," Ranji told him.

The Superus bit at it. It was as tough as the sole of a shoe, and so bitter, his mouth gathered up as if it had been stitched with a linen thread and the thread drawn tight.

"Pffooff!" he cried, spitting it out the best he could. "Yoof poithontht me!"

"Oh, not at all," Ranji said cheerfully. "Though it may have the cleansing effect of a purge on you if you eat much of it, it won't kill you. I've never seen anyone die of it. But come to think of it, I'd advise you to eat no more, for I've never seen anyone take more than one bite."

"You said the peasants ate it," growled the Superus.

"I said they tried to eat it," Ranji corrected him. "But only when there was nothing else in all the world for them to eat."

The Superus sighed. "I wish I had my burned carrot."

"I'll see what I can do," said Ranji, all sympathy.

12

The Second Hundred Days

Every day, after his breakfast of rice and whey, the Superus lifted his head to sniff at the tantalizing odors of four hundred delectable breakfast dishes and weep—from joy, of course.

One day he pushed himself to his feet and went to the window, where he stared out into the garden of the courtyard. A strange look suddenly crossed his face.

"Why am I standing on my feet?" he asked Ranji.

"Why, because there is no one to carry you," Ranji told him.

"I thought I couldn't," the Superus said with a mixture of anger and wonder in his voice.

"Perhaps you were misinformed," Ranji told him.

The Superus scowled. "I will have them hanged for lying to me."

"Oh, do not do that, Mighty Superus. It was the duty of your servants to carry you. They wished only to serve you."

After that the Superus rose each day and paced the floor. He wrung his hands, knowing that he must wait until evening for his meager grains of rice. He counted the days between fish tails and burned carrots and dreamed of the goat cheese he would have on the twenty-ninth day.

One day Ranji said, "I have news. Ijnarini appeared before me as I was on my way to the kitchen. She told me that you must begin the second hundred days of living like a peasant." He looked at the Superus critically. "That means that unless you want to die tomorrow, you must learn to till the soil and plant as the peasants do.

"It is a happy day for you," the boy went on quickly, as he saw the clouds gathering on the face of the Superus, "for you stand on your feet, and it will be easy for you to spade and rake and plant and hoe and harvest good things to eat, as the peasants do."

He put the Superus to spading in the garden of the walled courtyard that lay beyond the window of the throne room.

"Fat, crunchy radishes come from these little round seeds. And *poori* comes from the wheat when you have harvested it," Ranji told him.

Now the Superus could well have been angry at doing such hard work, but the words *"poori"* and "radishes" stuck in his mind. He spaded and raked and planted the radish seeds and the grains of wheat.

One day, when Ranji wasn't looking, the Superus slipped the tail of a boiled fish into the ground along with the blackest end of a burned carrot, patted them down, and watered them carefully. Another day he carefully covered a crumb of goat cheese and tamped the rich soil over it.

One night he had visions of bowls of rice with gently seasoned carrots sliced on top all sprouting from vines that covered the ground; of *poori* growing on little bushes; of golden fried fish dangling from stalks like those of sugarcane; and of slabs of goat cheese nestled among the petals of hibiscus flowers. His mouth watered.

"The first to come," Ranji told him, "will be the radishes."

The Superus could scarcely keep himself from eating the tender green leaves that first poked through the soil.

"No, no!" Ranji cried. "You must wait for the crisp, tingling roots that will soon swell to a delicious size. Then you can eat them, leaves and all."

Each day the Superus watched anxiously, his mouth watering, his stomach rumbling. The fattening tops of the radishes were beginning to show.

One day Ranji said, "Tomorrow they will be ready."

The Superus could scarcely wait for morning to come. All night long he tossed and turned and dreamed of eating radishes, tailed root, crunchy bulb, stems, and leaves.

The next morning he rushed out to his garden.

"*Aaarrrow!*" His roar echoed through all the palace and a good portion of the fortress itself. "*Worrraaa!*"

Such a howl it was that Ranji rushed into the garden, the bowl with thirty-seven grains of rice in his hand.

"They are gone! The radishes are gone!" sobbed the Superus.

So they were. Every last one had been plucked. There was no trace of them at all. Not so much as a yellowed leaf was left.

"But this is impossible!" Ranji cried in dismay. "Who could have stolen them? No one can get into this garden but yourself!"

The Superous roared and stamped and tore his hair. "I will hang the thief with my own hands!" he shouted.

Ranji shook his head, then clapped his hand to his forehead. "I shall see if I can find Ijnarini. She will know who has done this terrible thing!" Off he ran.

When he returned, he found the Superus sitting on his bench, still weeping of disappointment.

"Alas, Mighty Superus, Ijnarini has said that there is only one thing that can have happened. But first I must ask you. What did you dream about last night?"

"I dreamed of eating radishes," the Superus wailed.

Ranji nodded. "Just so. And that is what happened. You rose in your sleep and ate your radishes. Tell me, did you enjoy them?"

The Superus groaned. "I thought I did. But I am as hungry as ever."

Ranji shook his head in sympathy. "Radishes are

not very filling. But you must be of good cheer, for you know that the peasants never get to eat their radishes, even in their dreams. They have always had to pull them and send them directly to your kitchen. At least you have had the pleasure of eating yours during your dream."

This alarmed the Superus. "Do you think I will die tomorrow?"

"I don't know," Ranji said thoughtfully. "We can only wait and see. It does not seem fair that you be held responsible for your dreams." He shook his head sorrowfully.

They sat side by side on a bench in the garden, the Superus sighing and now and again wiping away a tear.

Finally Ranji said, "Who knows? *Perhaps,* now and then, when a peasant has dreamed of eating them, he did so in his sleep, just as you did. I am sure that even if it has happened only once from the very beginning of time, it would save you from death. Especially if you forgave that peasant in your heart."

The Superus wiped away at his now fast-coming tears. "Oh, I do, I do!" he cried.

The Most Excellent One did not die the next day. He silently blessed the peasant who must also have eaten his dream, and said to Ranji, "I hope the peasants eat more of their dreams."

The days passed. Every other night Ranji trimmed and stitched up the clothes of the Superus so he would not notice how much thinner he was becoming. Every day the Superus watched as the wheat became taller and then as the grains at the top began to swell.

"When the *poori* is ripe, I shall sit up all night and watch that no one steals it," he said grimly, "even myself!"

Beards grew on the wheat, and the Superus watched carefully for the *poori* to start appearing. Surely they would start as small cakes and grow larger and fatter, as the radishes had.

Ranji told him, "Tomorrow the wheat will be ready to harvest."

The Superus did not quite believe him. There was no sign of *poori* hanging from the slender stalks. Even so, he stood at his window and looked into his garden, feeling a stir of pride that it was so well kept. For he had hoed and weeded, and the stalks stood straight and golden with just their heads bending in the slight breeze. He would sit up all night tonight, for it must be that the *pooris* would burst forth from those heavy nodding heads.

But as he watched, a cloud suddenly darkened the garden. Looking up, the Superus saw a flock of crows wheeling overhead. Having no idea what this might mean, he stood and watched, amazed that so many birds would flock together.

Then the crows descended.

Alas! By the time the Superus realized what was happening, it was too late. Even as he rushed from the door, the last black bird rose and flapped away. Not a grain of wheat was left.

Oh, there was never such a raging, roaring, and shrieking, stamping, and flailing of arms as Ranji beheld when he rushed into the garden after the Superus. Surely no one before or since has ever witnessed such a fury as that of the Highest Most Excellent One when he saw that no hope for a single *poori* was left him. He leaped up and down, rent his shirt from neck to navel, tore it into seven pieces, tossed the shredded rags into the air, and then threw himself down and beat the ground with his fists.

Ranji surveyed all and shook his head in dismay.

"Well," he sighed when the Superus had grown too hoarse to make another sound and too tired to kick the earth one more time, "you should consider yourself lucky. Crows often eat the crops of the peasants, so you are most certainly living like a peasant."

13

The Next
Ninety-Seven Days

anji's words did little to comfort the Superus
for the loss of his puffy little golden *pooris*.
"There is one thing that you may reap from this,"
the youth told him as he finally helped the Excellent
One to his feet and brushed him off. "Unless the donkeys eat the straw, the peasants use the dried stalks
to make a pillow for their heads."

The boy picked up the shreds of the Superus's shirt.
"We will stitch this into a pillow that you can stuff
with the straw. You will have something to put under
your head when you sleep."

Indeed, the Superus had been complaining even
more about the hardness of his bed, because much of
the natural cushion with which he had been endowed
was disappearing, and here and there a bone ground
uncomfortably against the stone of the bench. More
and more often he had asked Ranji about the beds of
the peasants. Ranji always answered the same. The
peasants slept on mats on the floor, but as the marble
floor of the Superus's palace was as hard as the stone

bench, it would make little difference to him where he chose to place his mat. It was certainly easier for Ranji to help the Superus rise from the bench than from the floor.

So when at last the Superus recovered from pouting, Ranji showed him how to stitch the pieces of cloth into a pillow and stuff it with dried wheat stalks. The night it was finished, the Superus put it under his head. Never had a pillow with a silken cover stuffed with the finest down of white ducks felt as soft.

The next morning the Superus sniffed and pouted. "I don't have a shirt. Don't the peasants wear shirts?"

"They sometimes wear a shirt. Well, more often a kind of tunic," Ranji said thoughtfully. "I'll find something for you."

The boy went off at once to the seamstress and returned to the Superus with a square of coarse cotton cloth. He tore a strip from one end of it and then cut a hole in the middle.

"Put your head through the hole, and we shall belt it at the waist with this strip of cloth. You will be a well-dressed peasant then."

The Superus sighed. The cloth was not the soft silk and satin that he was used to. It was scratchy and rough around his neck, but what was there to say? At least there was an ease to moving his arms that he had not had with the most elegant of his tight-fitting silken shirts that were embroidered with heavy gold thread.

"What would the Superani think of such a peasant for a husband!" he growled. "It is a good thing she has never seen me and never will."

It was the first time he had ever mentioned the Superani.

"Did she not see you even on your wedding day?" Ranji asked.

"Yes. But we were only children. She was a skinny little girl of seven. A pest and a tease." The Superus scowled fiercely. "She insulted me so, that once the wedding ceremony was over, I had her locked away where she would never bother me again with her impudence."

Ranji nodded. "Children of seven are often guilty of being impudent."

The Superus's face grew darker yet. Suddenly the words burst from him. "She called me fatso! I was no more than pleasingly plump at the age of ten! To spite her, I ate seventeen cakes on our wedding day. To spite her, I have been eating as much as the cooks can cook ever since that day."

Ranji's lips quivered. He shook his head and turned his face aside. He swallowed. He could scarcely keep his laughter quiet. When he was certain his voice would not tremble, he asked, "So since the wedding you have not seen her any more than she has seen you?"

"No."

"Hmmm. I wonder what she looks like now?" Ranji

murmured. "A superani is certain to be the most beautiful woman in the land."

"Hmmp!" snorted the Superus, and said no more.

* * *

One day the Superus leaned over and put on his sandals.

Another day he glanced at the floor and, without bending forward, saw his own toes. Not only that, he could lean down and touch those toes without gasping for breath.

"Why is this so?" he asked Ranji.

"It comes of living like a peasant," Ranji told him. "Though most of them go barefoot, they can all lean over without gasping for breath. It is a way they have. That you can do it is the best of news!"

"I can't understand that I learned to do it without your telling me how," said the Superus.

"It is indeed a wonder!" Ranji shook his head in awe.

Ranji now made the Mighty One walk around and around the walled courtyard, for, he said, the peasants walked many miles to work in their fields. One day he told the Superus, "You must learn to run, for the peasants run when a flood comes and they must flee their homes," adding, "so the calves of their legs are as hard as the stone of your bed."

"I have always hated to run," the Superus complained.

"It must be done," Ranji insisted.

"It will be the death of me," whined the Mighty One.

"Oh, on the contrary!" Ranji disagreed. "And remember, tomorrow comes only once."

The Highest Most Excellent Superus sulked. Even so, at first only at a fast walk, then at a jog-trot, and finally at a full-blown run, the Superus went around and around his garden.

"Hiya!" Ranji cried. "Faster yet! The flood is at your heels!"

"It wouldn't be so bad if my pants weren't so tight," the Superus growled one day as he came to a halt, huffing and puffing.

"Perhaps we should let out the seams," Ranji suggested.

"There's not enough to let out," the Superus said on examining the inside seams.

Ranji shook his head. "What a pity!"

"When this three hundred days is at an end, it will be almost time for another hanging." The Superus sat down to his usual bowl of thirty-seven grains of rice. "There will be no question for me in deciding who it will be. I will have the best of all seamstresses hanged for making such narrow seams."

"Hmmm," Ranji mused, and offered him the burned carrot. "Do you mean there is sometimes a question about a hanging?"

The Superus scowled and swallowed the burned carrot whole.

"There is always a question. I hate hangings. They

make me feel ill. That is why I have to eat twice as much after each one. It helps settle my stomach." He took up the bowl and licked it, though there was nothing there to lap up. "Only usually I feel worse after eating twice as much."

"Then why do you have the hangings, O Mighty Superus?" Ranji asked.

"It is the custom."

"Hmmm," Ranji said again. "How is it you choose who is to be hanged?"

"I usually choose the one I like the best. It makes me feel so much worse that I have to eat that much more."

Ranji did not know what to say to this.

"That is why I chose that dancer," the Superus went on gloomily. "I have always wanted to dance, but how could I? I thought I couldn't even stand on my feet. So I watched others dance. I hated them for being able to dance so well, but I loved to watch them all the same. He was the best I had ever seen. What else was I to do but have him hanged?" Suddenly he glared at Ranji. "Now look what you've done! Talking about this has made me swallow the carrot without savoring it!"

"I'm sure you did the right thing in ordering him to be hanged," Ranji soothed him, ignoring the matter of the carrot. An idea was coming to him. "And it is the most important thing in the world that you told me of this, for there is something I had to tell you and did not know how to say it. Now I know. The thing is this. You must learn to dance. Ijnarini herself has informed me of it.

"All the peasants know how to dance," he went on quickly, for the Superus's scowling face was beginning to resemble the underside of a thundercloud. "Many of the dances you have watched have come from the most ancient dances of the peasants. We cannot wait another day to start. Today you must begin to dance for your life."

"I told you I could never dance because I could not stand on my feet!" the Superus repeated, slouching back on his bench.

"Ah, but now you can!" Ranji said, and drew the Superus to his feet.

"That's true!" exclaimed the Superus. "I've been doing it for weeks, but you never spoke of dancing, only of running. Why is that?"

"You weren't ready yet to dance. It takes more effort than running. I think you will discover that yourself," Ranji said as he picked up the empty rice bowl. "Though we might have started sooner if you had told me how much you liked dancing."

"I was always so hungry, I hadn't thought about it." With a voice filled with gloom, the Superus added, "Hunger has a way of taking all my attention."

Ranji nodded. "It is so for the peasants, too."

"Miserable peasants!" growled the Superus. "If I had known I would have to live like them, I might have seen to it that they lived better."

"Ahhh," murmured Ranji. "That is something for you to remember."

"I cannot understand why I didn't know until now that I could stand and walk and run," the Mighty One went on, ignoring Ranji's remark.

"It is a marvel beyond *my* understanding, but I am one who never questions fortune," Ranji said humbly. "Let us be thankful that you know now, however, for it is surely a lucky thing. The peasants stand and walk and run all the time. And they dance, when they are not too tired. That you can do so too means that we can start at once with my teaching you the beginnings of dancing, and there will be no question of your not living like a peasant. I shall take your bowl to the kitchen and come back with my flute. You will dance for yourself and all the world by the time the next hundred days is up!"

Out the boy went.

14

The Last Three Days

"Oh, Phufadia! Who is to say what will happen now?" Ranji murmured to the night. "I have used all my wits. My bowl of mischief is empty. I cannot think what more Ijnarini would have the Superus do, so she is no longer of any use to me. I must devise an explanation of why she can never be found. I must convince the Superus that she would only babble nonsense into his ear.

"The Superus! O My Phufadia, his pants were too tight for dancing, so he now wears a long piece of cloth, which he winds around his shoulders and his waist and catches up between his legs and tucks in here and there. He loves so to dance, he swears he will never wear gold-embroidered cloth again!

"Still, he is the Superus and must appear so to his people. There are only three days left of the three hundred days, and no one has laid eyes upon him. He must soon appear before them, and he is much changed. How will they know he is truly himself? How will I keep from being hanged for this mischief? How, if I am hanged, will I be able to take your ashes to the great desert?"

It had been long since Ranji had heard the voice of Phufadia, and he did not expect to have an answer now. So he was much surprised when he heard the voice come in the night.

"Even if your bowl is empty, I do not doubt *you* are still full of mischief, for you are no less a scamp and an imp than you ever were." It was certainly the voice of the old faquir, though there was a dusty sound to it.

His ashes grow old with waiting, the boy thought with remorse, and replied, "So you have always told me."

"If Ijnarini cannot be found, perhaps you need a touch of magic" came the voice after a minute.

"Magic!" Ranji exclaimed. "Ah, if only I could bring about true magic, it would indeed be welcome!"

"Why can't you?"

"But . . ."

"Do you doubt your own mischief? You have gone on with your tricks for almost three hundred days."

"Mischief is not magic!"

"Ah, but it might be."

"Tell me!" Ranji cried aloud, and then stuffed his hand into his mouth.

But Phufadia did not tell him, and Ranji turned and turned on his mat. It was all his own doing that kept him uncomfortably awake, for now that the Superus was not so fat, he no longer snored thunder into the boy's ears.

But for all the youth's thinking, no answers came to him. Nor did a dream come to him.

The next morning the Superus pursed his lips and narrowed his eyes when Ranji set his rice before him. Then he asked, "What new step will you teach me today?"

"Alas," Ranji said. "I have taught you all I ever learned."

The Superus frowned. "Must I have you hanged for your ignorance?"

"O Mighty One, there are but three days left of the three hundred. While these are being accomplished, I will search for and find the best dancer who has ever danced in the land to teach you. Meanwhile we must think of how you are to be presented to your people, and how you are to be feasted! Surely you will want eight hundred dishes prepared for your first dinner. The cooks must be informed of your need."

"You will inform them. Meanwhile there are still three more days left, and I want to learn more dancing."

Ranji nodded miserably. He had hoped the thought of eight hundred delicacies would make the Superus forget about dancing. Now he searched frantically for another idea.

The Superus glared at him. "So, you are unable to teach me more?" he growled. "Then let me tell you something. You are a scamp and an imp and full of mischief."

"Am I indeed?" Ranji asked, startled.

"Yes," said the Superus with a frown that grew ever more threatening. "I was told that in a dream last night."

"Ah!" His breath left so suddenly that for once Ranji could form no words. But as the Superus continued to glare at him, "Who . . . who appeared to you to tell you this in your dream?" he managed to stammer.

"I have no idea who it was. It was a voice in the night. From its words, I feel that for the last two hundred and ninety-seven days you have somehow tricked me, though I don't yet know how."

Again Ranji was without words.

"No one tricks the Mighty Superus!" the Eminent One roared suddenly. "If what the voice said was true, in three days I will have you hanged for it! And the seamstress will be hanged for leaving no room to let out my pants, and the seventeen carriers who took me to and from my bed will be hanged for never letting me use my legs, and the twenty cooks and their twenty apprentices will be hanged for stuffing me so with good things to eat that I could not move, only not before they have prepared eight hundred dishes for me to enjoy after their demise. And the peasants will all be hanged for leading the miserable lives that I have had to emulate. And any others I decide to hang will be hanged! Yes! The Superani will be hanged, because she called me fatso and has borne me no children."

"Oh! Oh! Oh!" Ranji groaned, a thousand times more miserable than he had ever been in his life at the thought of the mischief he had brought about. "Why hang so many who are innocent of mischief and only wanted to serve you? Is it not enough to have me alone hanged?"

"No! For all of these others have made me miserable all of my life! And now I am hungry as I have never been hungry! As I can always eat more after a hanging, they will all be hanged, one by one! It will be a consummate celebration, lasting for as many days as there are hangings! It may be that I shall celebrate for three hundred days!"

"O Mighty Superus!" Ranji cried, throwing himself to the floor and covering his head with his hands. "All the mischief of the past two hundred and ninety-seven days was indeed of my own doing. Take my own wretched life, but I beg you spare the others! They are truly innocent of any wrongdoing! They only wished to serve you! Even the Superani! Surely she loves you, for a seven-year-old girl always teases most the one she loves best. Surely she now regrets calling you fatso, and how could she bear your children if she does not have you for a father to them? Spare her! Spare them all! Let me do something for you that will make you change your mind about them! Command me! I will do anything!"

The Superus continued to glare at Ranji. "Well," he admitted after a time, "there were a few other words in my dream."

"Tell me, O Mighty Superus!"

"You must do a magic from your mischief," said the Superus.

"There is nothing I would do more gladly!" Ranji exclaimed, wondering desperately what magic he might do.

"Very well," said the Superus with a loud snuffing of his nose. "There are two things I want, so do these, Master Mischief Maker. Do these with your magic! First! Bring Ijnarini to me. I will hear the end of that tale. Second! You promised you would bring the best dancer who ever danced in this country to be my teacher. Look to your words and do so, or be hanged. But know this! It will have to be magic indeed and no trick, you scamp and imp, for from my dream I gathered that Ijnarini is nowhere to be found. As for the best dancer who ever danced in this country— you know as well as I that he was hanged last year."

15

And Then

anji hastened to call the servants to collect the trays of food from behind the palace wall and bring them to the kitchen.

"So!" he murmured to himself. "I have been ordered to make magic from mischief, first by my dear Phufadia, then from the Superus himself. Aha! Well! It may not be so hard a thing as I first thought!" He hurried to the kitchen after the servants.

"You must start preparing eight hundred dishes for the Superus so that they are ready three days from now," he told the twenty cooks and their twenty apprentices.

There was a loud cry, and they clustered around the youth. "Is there to be a hanging?" they asked.

"Who is to say?" Ranji answered. "The Superus has ordered that all his subjects appear before him on that day—servants, cooks, guards, entertainers, the peasants from the village—everyone! Including even the Superani!"

"Ahhh!" exclaimed all the cooks and their apprentices in a breath so great, seven cook fires were blown out.

"I can tell you no more, because that is all I know, and I have much to do. Give me but one taste before I go!"

The boy sampled three dishes from the simmering pots and then was off and running.

First he went to the best of all seamstresses, giving measurements to her that were completely new. She would have argued long and hard. "Who is there in the palace who could wear such clothes?"

Ranji was firm. "You will do as I say! The Superus orders it!"

"Aaiii! What a stubborn one you are!" snorted the seamstress.

"True!" Ranji agreed, and he hurried away.

Next he went to the youngest and most beautiful of the girl dancers. He took her hands in his and looked wistfully into her bewitching eyes. He told her she must prepare herself to appear before the Eminent One in three days, then added, "You must of course dance and dance and dance—all of the dances you used to dance with Chahansa you must practice for this whole three days in preparation. There may even be one to dance with you then! Who is to say how many lives depend upon it?"

"Oh, I will! *We* will! All of us. Thank you, dear Ranji!" Her smile was radiant. She threw her arms around him and hugged him and thanked him and then ran off to begin her practicing.

Ranji sighed. "Ah, well," he murmured to himself. "It was nice to be hugged so tightly, even if it was only this once."

He then hurried to the far end of the palace where he might give instructions through the marble grille of the window of the quarters of the Superani.

"She will come before the Superus in three days. See to it that she is so beautifully dressed she eclipses the moon and the stars," Ranji informed the old-woman servant on the other side of the window.

"Moon and stars indeed! How little you know of these things!" snorted the old woman. "It will be enough if we can keep her from weeping her eyes to redness with this order! She has heard what sort of man the Superus is! She knows well enough the sentence under which she is allowed to live only from day to day."

"There may be many surprises on *that* day," Ranji said. "Tell her the Superus orders her not to weep."

Last of all he spent forty-three minutes arguing with the eleven guards at the gate to the fortress. Finally, with Ranji's solemn vow that by the sacred ashes of his own beloved father he would return, they relented, and Ranji ran down the hill to the village to bring a summons to all who dwelt there, and to one in particular.

Out of breath and panting, the boy returned to the Superus, whose mood had not in the least lightened. The Mighty One paced his room like an angry tiger, or perhaps more like a hungry one. He glared at Ranji and swallowed all thirty-seven grains of rice at one bite. There was neither fish head nor carrot this day to distract him.

Finally Ranji reminded him, "O Mighty Superus, you have only two and one half days to continue the life of a peasant! Surely after living through so many, you do not wish to die on the very last of those three hundred days because you behaved like a Superus rather than a peasant!"

"Bah!" shouted the Superus. "Now that I know you are a scamp and an imp and full of mischief, how do I know that all of these three hundred days were not of your own invention? How do I know that peasants have only thirty-seven grains of rice at a meal? How do I know that they dance? How do I know that they dream of radishes or have crows eat their *pooris*? It is only because you have told me so! What I really know is that I am hungrier today than I have ever been in my life! And angrier! I know what it is to want to hang all who appear before me!"

"Ah, Mighty One, such things may or may not be so, but how do you know without doubt that the words of Ijnarini were not as immutably true as the order of the stars in the heavens? The only way to find out carries a chance of invoking a certain finality."

"Hmmp!" The Superus sat down and drummed his fingers on the stone bench. "Ijnarini!" he shouted suddenly. "She promised me the end of the story of the golden bird."

"Not until the three hundred days have been accomplished," Ranji reminded him.

"How do I know she will keep her promise if she is not to be found?"

"I will search the palace and the fortress for her," Ranji promised.

"You will stay here and serve me," growled the Superus. "I want to keep an eye on you!"

This day was not an easy one for Ranji. Even tricks and stories did not appease the Superus. An occasional bellow from the Mighty One assured the rest of the palace that the Superus was still very much himself in spite of his ordeal, whatever it had been—perhaps that of going without his noonday meal. Of course, the roaring did little to comfort Ranji, and the hours stretched to three times their usual length for the boy. But that day finally came to an end, with the sun setting as it always did.

The next day was even more difficult. The Mighty Superus roared and raged as he paced around and around his the room. His threats of hangings to come made Ranji tremble. It was only through the boy's repeated reminders of Ijnarini's warning that kept the Superus from breaking his promise.

Night came at last.

"O My Beloved Faquir," Ranji whispered to the darkness, "why did you let the Mighty One hear your voice when you spoke to me? I have done and am doing all I know how to do, and I hope for the best, but I have a great fear of the consequences. These past two hundred and ninety-nine days have been a great penance for me, but they were clearly not enough. The Mighty Superus is almost sure he has found me out. There is not a moment now that I do not wish I had taken your ashes at once to the great desert and never stopped to taste in the kitchen of the Superus!"

There was no comforting reply from Phufadia.

"I suppose I am the maker of my own fate," Ranji at last whispered to himself. And a moment later, "No, on the contrary, I am not the maker of my own fate, dear Phufadia. For did you not say I was born an imp and a scamp and full of mischief? How is such a thing to be changed? Would I not be false to myself and to everyone else if I tried some other face than my own delightful one? The fearful mask of the hangman? The oily mask of the politician? Must I not do the best I can with what I am?"

There was still no answer.

"Tell me, Phufadia, if I were a true imp, would I not take your ashes and steal away this very night through the back door of the palace? It lies at my right hand and waits only for me to open it."

Again silence. Ranji sighed.

"You give me neither yes nor no. If I am to know nothing, I am to know nothing. If I am to understand nothing, I am to understand nothing. So I must decide it all in my own head. No. I cannot run away tonight.

There are too many who might be hanged if I did, and it would all be my fault. Now that I have decided to stay, it is written that in two days I will either resume my journey and take your ashes to the great desert to scatter them beneath the branches of the barren thornbush, or I will be hanged."

With that, Ranji closed his eyes and fell asleep and slept deeply with no dreams.

Perhaps the Superus too slept deeply, for all of the next day—the three hundredth day—he was strangely silent.

16

The Three Hundred and First Day

It started at one minute past midnight of the three hundred and first day—the greatest hubbub that had ever been known in the palace of the Superus, or in all of the fortress, or in the kingdom, or perhaps even in all of that ancient land. Servants rushed to and fro. Tall guards clanked their curved swords and twisted the ends of their mustaches into great flourishing curls. The carriers of the Superus flexed their muscles. The seamstresses stitched frantically, cooks cooked, music sounded, dancers danced for each other, entertainers entertained each other, all in preparation and practice for the dawn of the three hundred and first day since the Superus had mysteriously gone into seclusion.

For every one of those three hundred days everyone had wondered why he had done so, but no one but the Superus knew. No one but the Superus and Ranji. No one but the Superus and Ranji and Ijnarini. But no one had ever been able to find Ijnarini to ask her. Ranji had been asked but would not speak of it. And even if he *could* have done so, there was not one who would have dared ask the Superus.

And what of the Superus now that the time had passed?

At the instant of midnight he had retired to his bedroom, where Ranji had created a tent from the same piece of cloth the seamstress had made to cover the largest of the royal elephants. Beneath this the Great One slept in his own soft bed. No one knew how Ranji had managed to move him thither, but it had been done, and heads were shaken that a single youth could do such a thing. There must be magic involved in such a feat!

At one minute past midnight, workers swarmed through the palace and into the throne room. By the break of day the imperial room of the Superus was restored to its original magnificence. The stone bench was removed and the throne dragged back to its proper place and adorned with gems and the feathers of a peacock. The jewels were again set into the walls. The pool was filled with diamonds and emeralds, rubies and sapphires. The basins and jars overflowed with pearls and opals, carnelian and topaz. The table, itself a hundred paces around, was covered with a gold-threaded damask cloth laid with silver and gold platters, and soon to groan beneath the weight of eight hundred succulent dishes prepared by the twenty cooks and their apprentices.

By dawn all was ready.

The peasants from the village lined up at the gates, waiting to be let in so they too might attend the breakfast to celebrate the emergence of the Superus. They sang songs of praise for his courage in having endured three hundred days and of thanks for his generosity.

"Whatever *that* might have been," muttered those who dwelt in the fortress.

One from the village was let through the gate. He had been told that he must add his own special ability to the entertainment provided the Superus in this celebration. There were certain things that he must do to prepare himself. He was shown to Ranji's own room.

And Ranji, who was a scamp and an imp and full of mischief?

He again waited on the Superus, though the time was up that no one but the boy must keep his company. For this one day more the Superus refused the help of the usual servants who had last dressed him over three hundred days ago.

Basins of scented water were brought to the door of the Superus's bedroom, that the Most Excellent One might be bathed and perfumed. Ointments were brought that he might be anointed.

The usual bathers and anointers shook their heads when they heard the roars of the Superus. The boy was unskilled at such labors. Surely he would be hanged, and they along with him for not attending to their duties.

Then a magnificent suit of clothes was brought to the door and handed to Ranji.

The next moment there came such a raging howl from the bedroom of the Highest Most Excellent One that it was heard through all the fortress. The best of all the seamstresses set her lips and crossed her arms and scowled. Then her lips loosened and trembled.

"I told him so!" she wailed. "Even though I left seams so deep they could be let out to double the width, the clothes still will not fit the Mighty Superus! I shall be hanged for this." Tears ran down her cheeks.

But after a time the howling subsided.

Then the order came, through Ranji of course, that the eight hundred dishes must be set upon the table. When that was accomplished, the order came that all must leave the throne room until called for.

Again there was wonder and consternation and questions and the wildest of surmises. But there was nothing anyone could do but wait.

At last the order came that the Superus was prepared to have his breakfast and be amused. This was as it had always been, but this time the celebration was to be even more lavish, for all in the palace were to pass through the room and welcome the Superus back to his place upon the throne.

In came the prime ministers and the secretariat-wallahs, the sufis and the pongyis, the prophets and the gurus, the pundits and the poets, the barbers and the serving boys, the bathers and the carriers, the cooks and their apprentices, the musicians and the dancers, the seamstresses and the tailors, the guards and the hangman and all the others who dwelt within the fortress and were too numerous to name. All threw themselves to the floor before the Mighty Superus, cried their welcome to him, and then rose to back away and stare discreetly.

With a growl the Superus informed the seven men who leaped to bring him tidbits that he was not yet ready to partake of his breakfast, and so, filled with wonder, they too stood aside.

There was little different about the Superus that anyone could see, for he was draped from cheekbones to floor with the largest piece of cloth the seamstress had ever stitched to cover the largest of the royal elephants. But the little difference that those of the court could see was remarked upon. The eyes of the Superus seemed larger and brighter, and his nose sharper.

Then the villagers trooped through, again praising him and thanking him. None of them had ever been in the throne room, and they were overwhelmed by the majesty of it all. It took little effort for them to fall to their knees, for their knees were knocking together.

None of them had ever seen the Superus, so there was no difference for them to remark upon. But the Superus took stock of them, leaned sidewise, and remarked to Ranji, in a voice so low and muffled through the heavy elephant cloth that no one but the boy heard, "They are a healthy-looking lot and surely live on more than thirty-seven grains of rice a day!"

"Ah," Ranji murmured. "Do not forget the carrot and boiled head and tail of a fish!"

"What happens to that part of the fish that lies between the head and the tail?" asked the Superus.

Ranji bowed low and whispered, "Perhaps it is that part which you went without that they have partaken of for the past three hundred days. Perhaps that is why they look so healthy."

"Hmmm," said the Superus, glaring at Ranji with narrowed eyes.

At the very last the Superani appeared with her women clustered about her. The Superus motioned for the women to move aside, and the Superani was left alone, standing before the Superus.

"Ahhh!" The breath left all who looked upon her.

Was she beautiful?

Oh, but she was dazzling! Was it the silken garment of crimson and azure and gold? Was it the jeweled chains that sparkled around her neck and shoulders? Was it the bracelets of gold upon her arms? The sapphires at her ears? The delicate diamond at the side of her nose? The circlet of emeralds upon her brow? Were these what dazzled the eyes of all?

Or was it the thick-lashed, large dark eyes with the beauty spot next them that drew all looks to hers? Was it the delicate but well-shaped nose? The full and perfectly formed lips? The exquisite ears? The serene brow? The silky-smooth complexion? The glossy black hair? The proud lift of her head? The graceful figure?

"Ohhh!" Again a breath from all who crowded the room. Who could say what there was of the Superani that was not radiantly beautiful?

All the same, she was pale and still. She did not smile as she looked upon the Superus, who sat draped from cheekbones to floor with the heavy cloth woven and stitched together to cover the largest of the royal elephants. But look she did.

And look he did.

It seemed forever that the eyes of the Superus and those of the Superani were locked. And then . . .

"Ohhhahhhohhh!"

For the Superus had risen to his feet and thrown aside the heaviest cloth ever woven and stitched together to cover the largest of the royal elephants. He stood before all, in the most glorious raiment the weavers had ever woven and the seamstresses had ever stitched. There stood the Superus, the tallest, strongest, most handsome of Mighty Ones that anyone had ever supposed or pretended or fancied or thought or imagined or dreamed or seen or could possibly want.

17

What Happened Next

It was clear that the Superani saw and knew and understood at once all of what the Superus had become.

It was also clear that the Superus had seen and recognized and delighted in the exquisite perfection of the Superani before he even stood up.

He stepped down from the royal dais and stretched out his hand. The Superani took one step forward and reached out to rest her fingertips on the back of his hand. The Mighty One led her to the throne. There they stood one beside the other, and the Highest Most Excellent Superus, his eyes never leaving the face of the Superani, announced, "Now it is time we broke our fast. Now we will be amused."

Never was there such feasting in the whole history of the palace, or the fortress, or the superdom, or perhaps of that entire ancient land. The feasting was done by all except the Superus and the Superani, who indulged in the most modest of meals, a bowl of rice and fruit. It was as much as the Superani ever had for her breakfast. But the Superus . . . had the sight of the Superani completely taken his appetite for ordinary food—however extraordinary it might be—from him? Or was he so accustomed to the thirty-seven grains of rice that he was not hungry?

Whatever the reason, he feasted only with his eyes, and those fed upon the look of the Superani. When their fingers touched, the look of the Superus grew tender as it had never been and his voice grew gentle as it had never been. It was clear that his appetite was now all in his heart and would be satisfied only by the Superani.

During and after and again during feasting there was entertainment. Never was there such entertainment in the whole history of the palace, or the fortress, or the superdom, or perhaps of that entire ancient land. It was of such magnificence that all watched in ever greater delight. Even the Superus and the Superani watched now and then, when they were not lost in looking at each other.

The musicians played and the singers sang. The poets and the storytellers recited their best verses and stories. The villagers danced their peasant dances, for indeed they did have their dances and the Superus remarked that they danced them well. The palace dancers danced their court dances, with the youngest and most beautiful of the girl dancers dancing as she never had before. She whirled and twirled, and her eyes looked this way and that as they had never done before, and the bells on her ankles rang and her fingers snapped as they had never rung nor snapped before.

All of the day passed and the evening came and still the feasting and entertainment went on. Night fell and the light of the moon sifted through the windows and spread a silver patina upon the floor whereon lay the black tracing of the marble filigree, and still the feasting and the entertainment went on.

At last a moment of rest came. Suddenly the Superus shook himself and sat straight.

"Ranji!" he shouted, and everyone grew still. "Where is that imp and scamp and mischief maker known as Ranji!" roared the Superus, in his old, well-known voice. "He has not fulfilled his promises!"

Everyone looked around. For where had Ranji been all of this long day and evening that had lasted into the night?

It was simple enough. He too had feasted, though not in the way he used to do. And he too had watched the dancers and listened to the sound of the tabla and the sitar and the flute. He too had heard the poets and the storytellers. But it was always with a care to keep out of sight of the Superus. Indeed, at one moment he had slipped away from the celebration to go somewhere to whisper something to someone, and at another moment to go to his room and whisper to the ashes of Phufadia.

"O Beloved Faquir! All has come about in a way

much better than I had ever dreamed possible, or had *even* dreamed possible. Should you and I slip away now?"

The ashes did not speak to him.

"I would, except there is still some unfinished bit of mischief, and I fear the Superus would cause me trouble by sending after me."

Then he thought the voice of Phufadia did come to him. "Never leave unfinished mischief," it said. But Ranji was not certain if it was the true voice of the old faquir or only his own remembrance of it. Either way, it was an answer. The boy sighed and returned to the festivities. Now the Superus was calling for him.

Ranji came forward and bowed low, even falling to his knees and touching his forehead to the floor.

"I am at your command, O Mighty Superus!"

"I asked two things of you," said the Superus sternly, frowning all the while. "I have seen no sign of either of them."

"There was much to take your attention, O Most Excellent One," said the boy.

"I want them now!" commanded the Superus. "Or the hanging I promised you will take place! One hanging a year is still the custom!"

Ranji rose to his feet, pressed his palms together, and bowed his head.

"I will do my best, O Mighty One. Give me but a moment to gather my magic from my room, and I will do what I can."

"Watch him!" the Superus ordered the tallest of the guards, whose turban towered above all others and whose mustaches curled in the grandest fashion. "Do not let him leave the palace!"

Ranji gave the Superus a look of the greatest hurt imaginable. How could it be that the Mighty One did not trust him? But clearly he didn't, and Ranji was escorted to his room.

As far as the guard could see, the boy gathered only a few things—a jar, a handful of something, and a sack that appeared to be filled with rags. Then he spoke to the air.

"Come behind us softly, O magic one," he said. "The moment has come." Then Ranji informed the tall guard whose curved sword gleamed at his side, "You must not look back lest the power of magic overcome you."

Though the guard heard nothing coming behind him, his scalp beneath his turban prickled all the way from Ranji's room back to the throne room and the festivities. Surely something followed them! He prodded Ranji with his sword. "Faster, if you please!"

In the wide archway to the throne room, Ranji paused. In less than a moment he was seen by all.

"Come forward!" ordered the Superus.

"I stand in the door between two worlds," Ranji declared in a hollow voice. The guard hastened into the room and rested himself against the wall.

"Your first wish, O Mighty One! I call upon the powers of Mischgic!" Ranji cried, lifted his arm high, and brought it down swiftly. There was a sudden flash of light, a clap like close-by thunder, and a cloud of green smoke. Scarcely had anyone time to cry out, though the Superus himself gasped, when from the cloud leaped the greatest dancer that ever had or ever would dance in the superdom.

Chahansa, dressed in gold and crimson, leaped and twirled and whirled. And when all thought he must drop from exhaustion, he was joined by the youngest and most beautiful of the girl dancers, and they leaped and twirled and whirled, and her ankle bells rang and the music played. Then they were joined by all the dancers, who leaped and whirled and twirled. There was again the beat of the tabla and the thrilling melody of the flutes and the plucking of the sitars. At the last the peasants at the very back of the room joined in the dance with stamping and clapping.

Astounded and delighted, the Superus watched.

With mouths agape, all watched.

When it was over at last, Chahansa bowed low. "I have come to teach you, O Mighty Superus," he said.

"Teach me? Teach me what?" For a moment the Superus looked startled. Then understanding came to his face, and then doubt. "Hmmm," he said, hesitating. "Hmmm. Well, perhaps I will be content to watch you. But you must dance for me—for us"—he took

the Superani's hand in his own—"forever! You and
that one." He pointed to the youngest and most beautiful of the girl dancers.

Chahansa and the most beautiful of the girl dancers
held hands and bowed. "It is our only desire, O Highest Most Excellent One!"

The Superus nodded. "Very well! And now I will
have my story. Ranji! My second demand!"

This time Ranji came to the center of the room,
dragging the sack behind him. He bowed humbly. "O
Greatest of All Excellent Superuses," he said meekly,
"if I am able to fulfill this second demand, may I beg
two favors of you?"

"Well?" growled the Superus.

"I made a vow and must carry it out. Will you allow
me to take the ashes of my beloved Phufadia to the
great desert?"

"Hmmm," said the Superus. "Well, I suppose that
would put an end to your making mischief here, if it
is mischief you have made. Hmmm. Well, perhaps.
After I have my story, I shall decide. And what is the
second favor you ask?"

Again Ranji bowed.

"If you are displeased with my fulfillment of your
second demand, I beg that you have me hanged, and
all others you henceforth hang for love, hanged only
as you hanged Chahansa the dancer."

"And how did I do that?" The Superus frowned.

"O Mighty Superus, only as one who is a scamp and

an imp and full of mischief would have his best friend hanged," Ranji said humbly.

"Ah?" questioned the Superus, frowning even more as he leaned forward.

"I beg you wait the explanation of that until you have had the end of the story of the golden bird," Ranji said.

"Very well." The Superus leaned back and patted the hand of the Superani. "Bring me Ijnarini!"

"O Mighty Superus! Once more I call upon the powers of Mischgic!" Ranji cried, and flung both arms into the air.

There was a double flash and two claps and a cloud of smoke twice as great as before. And when the smoke had cleared, there stood the old woman all dressed in rags and with her face modestly covered. Ijnarini stood before the Superus and the Superani. Ranji had disappeared.

"The end of the story," quavered the old woman. "Very well, for you have fulfilled the choice you made for your three hundred days. Here it is then.

"The golden bird screeched with fright when the greedy thief reached for her. With that screech there came from her beak a dark cloud of smoke that brought cinders and blindness to the thief's eyes. Scarcely had he rubbed and blinked them away when there emerged from the smoke a monstrous winged creature. It had the eyes and shoulders of a vulture. The tips of its wings were sharpened arrows. Its talons were a hundred times the size of an eagle's and a hundred times sharper than the tiger's claws. Its beak was curved, and gleamed as fiercely as the scimitars of the guards at the gates of the abode of Shamshana-Kali.

"The greedy thief shrieked and fell back in terror, but he could not escape this fearsome bird. It seized his arms with its claws and caught his neck in its beak. Then it rushed him from the cave, breaking away the rock to the entrance so that light streamed in to the very back of the dark cavern. Soaring out over the deep chasm, the monster circled higher and higher until at last it dropped the thief, who fell and fell to the distant rocks below. That was the end of him.

"The golden bird, seeing the light of the opening, flew from the cave and straight into the air, it too rising higher and higher until it vanished into the sun itself, where it now and forever dwells."

Ijnarini fell silent.

"Go on," demanded the Superus.

"That's all there is," Ijnarini said with a shrug.

"That's all? There should have been something more. I'm disappointed. Where did that monstrous bird come from? What about the King? You're not such a good storyteller after all!"

"Oh, the King had to get along without the bird. He found musicians to sing and play for him. Of course jewels did not come from their mouths, but the sound of their instruments was pleasant. And the peasants had to work in the fields, but they had always done that, or there would have been nothing for anyone to eat. If there were no jewels, there was as much as ever of what was truly needed for all. No one suffered the lack of rice or clothes or a roof against the rains. The peasants brought to the palace what the King needed of their harvest. He protected them with his army and gave them music to dance to. As no one had ever learned to be greedy and they all cared for one another, they were as happy as they had ever been."

The Superus rubbed his chin.

"Still not satisfied?" Ijnarini asked impatiently. "Ah! The monstrous bird! You are a little slow. Everyone knows good and bad can come from the same heart. As long as the bird was loved, it was loving. But rouse fear and hatred, and you have a monster. Surely you know that? Do you want me to spell out even more of a moral? Something about not needing piles of one thing or another, whether jewels or power or whatever, to be happy? Surely you know that it is loving and caring for others that make the skies turn.

"Or do you want something more for your very own self? Something about a full stomach always feeling empty if it is not kept company by a full heart? Something about the greed of one forever begetting misery in others. Something about—"

"Stop! Stop! I hate morals tacked to the end of stories!" cried the Superus.

"Well then, what do you want?"

The Superus scowled and pouted. "I want to know in what way the dancer was hanged."

"Oh, that! Only like this!" And Ijnarini dumped onto the floor the contents of the sack Ranji had dragged behind him. They appeared to be a bundle of clothes, but when she picked the bundle up and shook it out, it was a puppet the size of a boy. It wore the clothes Chahansa had danced in the year before and had the mask of Chahansa for a face.

"It was this dancer you had hanged. It danced well enough at the end of the rope, but it never did and never will dance on its own two legs."

The Superus stared long at the puppet. "Ah," he said at last. "Truly the work of a scamp and an imp and one who is full of mischief. Where is he? Ranji!"

But Ranji did not answer.

It seemed the boy was not in the room. Everyone was immediately sent to search for him. At last the first cook's apprentice found him. Or rather, the apprentice found a puppet the size of a boy with Ranji's clothes and Ranji's face sitting on a shelf in the kitchen with a hand in a large cook pot. When the Superus was informed of this, he began to pout and scowl, but the Superani whispered to him and then she began to laugh. She laughed until tears ran down her face. She laughed so that others laughed, and it was in only two minutes that the Superus too burst out in laughter. He neither coughed nor choked, for there was no crumb in his mouth to bring on such a spell.

"So be it!" he cried. "When I make up my mind to have him hanged, I will do so. Whenever I am out of sorts, I shall have the same done again next year, and the year after that. In time perhaps it will even become the custom. Now, Ijnarini! I would have a word with you!" he cried.

But Ijnarini too had disappeared.

The Superus again pouted and started to scowl, but the Superani whispered to him.

"But *why* did Ijnarini have to go with him?" the Superus protested. "We could have listened to her stories forever, if only she would not point out morals."

A third time the Superani whispered to him.

"Do you really think so?" asked the Superus, much surprised. "One and the same? That . . . scamp!"

* * *

Whether Ranji found the barren thornbush no one in the land of the Superus ever found out, for he never returned to the country of that Mighty Most Excellent One to tell them. Rumor did come from the Kingdom of Hashgon, where the Satrap there was so fond of horses that his unhappy people suffered terrible deprivations. The rumor was that the most surprising events occurred after the arrival of a boy who was a scamp and an imp and full of mischief.

But in the Superdom of the Mighty Most Excellent Superus, all the people were happy, for their wise monarch well knew the meaning of both a full stomach and a full heart, and saw to it that all had a share of each.

About the Author

Ellen Kindt McKenzie lives in the San Francisco Bay Area of California and spends her summers in rural Wisconsin. She is the author of several books for young readers, including *Taash and the Jesters,* an ALA Notable Book; *The King, the Princess, and the Tinker,* a 1992 *American Bookseller* Pick of the Lists; and *Stargone John,* a *Bulletin of the Center for Children's Books* Blue Ribbon Book and winner of the Bay Area Book Reviewers Award for 1991.